21.95

# GRANDMA, DO PREACHERS LIE?

## A Guide to Truth for Youth

Connie Wiedeman

PublishAmerica
Baltimore

ISBN: 1-4137-6550-5
PUBLISHED BY PUBLISHAMERICA, LLLP
www.publishamerica.com
Baltimore

Printed in the United States of America

## Introduction

God has told us that we are responsible, not only for learning the truth, but for teaching others the consequences of not doing so.

If we know that someone is sinning against God, we are to sound the warning that this will result in that person's eternal death; to let him know that if he does not change his ways, he will die in his sins…and, having warned him, we will have saved our own eternal lives.

If we know that someone is sinning against God, but we do not warn him, his blood will be on our hands…we will be responsible for his eternal separation from God.

If we know that someone is sinning, warn him, but he refuses to heed the warning, he will still die in his sins, but his blood will not be on our hands.

I hope that this book will be a warning to all those who are following the sinful path of worshiping through false doctrines, that they are headed towards eternal death and will never see the Kingdom of God (Ezekiel: 33:7-9).

Dedicated with love to Breanna,
And in memory of my beloved son Craig

# Chapter 1
## The Immortal Soul and the Eternal Jesus

"…and if I die before I wake, I pray the Lord my soul to take. Amen."

They got up from their knees and Grandma held the covers while the young girl, barely a teenager, slithered into her warm bed. Her grandmother tucked her in just as she had done when she was a small child. Only her pretty face showed above the covers, and her grandmother kissed her protruding forehead. As she headed for the door and the light switch, she was followed by a question.

"Gammy, if I die in the night, will my soul go to heaven?"

Her grandmother dropped the hand that had been poised to extinguish the light and returned to the young girl's bedside.

"Where's the Bible I gave you for Christmas, Breanna?"

"Right there," she answered, pulling her arm from beneath the covers in order to point to the small chest just out of her reach.

Gammy reached and brought it to the girl without having to rise from the seat she'd taken on the bed.

"Here," she said, "find Ecclesiastes, chapter nine."

"O.K." She pushed herself up to a sitting position.

"Do you know where to find it?" Her grandmother reached toward the book.

"I can find it," Breanna exclaimed, clutching her Bible so that it couldn't be taken from her. While it took her a few tries to locate Ecclesiastes, she had made herself familiar enough with those sixty-six books of her Bible to find it more quickly than her grandmother had expected.

"O K. I've got it."

"Read me verses five and six."

Clearing her throat and adjusting her posture as if to perform a theatrical piece, she began. *"'For the living know that they shall die; but the dead know nothing'."* She looked at her grandmother questioningly, but continued. *"'And they have no more reward, for the memory of them is forgotten'."* She paused again but her grandmother said nothing. *"'Also their love, their hatred and their envy have now perished; nevermore will they have a share in anything done under the sun'.* Gammy, what does perish mean?"

"It means to be destroyed or to pass away completely. So what does that verse say to you? Tell me in your own words."

Before she spoke, she paused, rereading the verse to herself.

"It says that after I'm dead I won't know anything. But, Gammy, the preacher told me that Grandpa was watching over me from heaven." She practically whined. "He says that when you're dead in this life, your soul is present with the Lord." She was clearly puzzled.

"I know. That's in second Corinthians, but first you ought to know exactly what you mean by your soul. In the very first book of the Bible…which one is that?"

"Genesis!" she said quickly, grinning with pride at her knowledge.

"Yes, right there in Genesis, when the Bible says that God made man out of the dust of the ground and breathed life into him, we are told that man became a living soul. Not that he *had* a soul, but that he *was* a soul."

"Where?" Breanna was fingering Genesis furiously.

"Try Chapter 2, verse 7."

"'*And the Lord God formed man of the dust of the ground, and breathed into his nostrils the breath of life; and man became a living being.*'" She looked questioningly at her grandmother.

"That's exactly what a soul is. A living being. A whole, living being. When God made man out of the dust, all He had was the form of a man…sort of like a statue. Not until God breathed life into that statue did it become a living person…a living soul. The King James translation of the Bible actually says, 'a living soul', but in recent years, the use of 'living being' appears to be more understandable, because that's exactly what 'a living soul' is. What people meant when they said body and soul was the physical body…like the original dust…and the life that was breathed into it."

"All my friends go to different churches and they all believe the soul is separate and goes to heaven. If the Bible doesn't say the soul is separate, then why do all the churches teach that it is?"

"Unfortunately, Honey, early in the life of Christianity, doctrines were contaminated by the Greeks. Teachings of such so-called great thinkers as Plato were introduced into church teachings. The subject of the immortality of the soul was one of those false teachings. The Bible is clear that such a belief is not a true doctrine.

"The word immortal or immortality doesn't appear but five times in the entire Bible. In 1 Timothy, chapter 6, verse 16, we are told that God alone has immortality. 2 Timothy 1, verse 10 points out that Jesus is the one who brought immortality to our attention when God raised Him from the dead; Romans 2, verse 7 tells us that we must seek for immortality, that it isn't something that we already have.

"1 Corinthians 15, verse 53 tells us that we will get immortality at the resurrection, and verse 54 confirms that the resurrection will be when Christ returns."

"Gammy, how do we seek immortality?"

"We must accept Jesus as our Savior, be baptized into His name and follow His commandments so that when we are raised from the dead, we will be given the immortality that is reserved for true believers."

This was not easy for Breanna to accept. Her entire, short life she had been taught that she had a soul that would live on after her death. "The Bible doesn't say the soul is separate?" She was still confused and hopeful.

"No, Honey, that's not what it says. Wait a second, I'll be right back."

She left the room and Breanna could hear her footsteps descending the stairs and a few seconds later, ascending less rapidly. When she entered the room, she had one of the books from Breanna's set of *Encyclopedia Britanica.*

"Sometimes you can get a more accurate meaning of a Bible word from sources other than those written by Bible scholars and theologians."

"You can?" She seemed surprised.

"Sometimes the people who interpret the Bible are influenced by their own beliefs, and the interpretations are then likewise influenced."

"You mean they lie about what really happens?"

"No, Sweetheart, I wouldn't say they *always* lie. Sometimes it's just that they see things differently because of what they already believe."

"Oh." It was pretty obvious that she didn't understand.

"When you said your prayers tonight, you asked God to take your soul to heaven if you died…"

"Uh huh."

"Well," she continued, "you asked for that because you had been told that your soul was separate from your body and that it lived on after you died. In other words, you were influenced in your prayer by what you already believed…what you had been taught."

"Why do they teach it in Sunday School if it isn't true?"

"Because many Sunday School teachers believe it's true. They are usually volunteers who are provided with pamphlets and papers that tell them what to teach. Personally, I believe they should study the Scriptures to determine the truth of what they are teaching, but for some reason, most feel no obligation to do that. In fact, I had a friend who was teaching a Sunday school class and was trying to teach from the Bible. Do you know what happened to him?"

"What?"

"He was removed as a teacher because they said he was teaching falsehoods."

"So what did he do?"

"Happily, he found himself another church. One that has built its doctrines on the Bible. While God makes no distinction between Sunday School teachers and preachers, I can't help but feel a little sorry for the Sunday School teachers who don't know any better, even though they should. But there is no excuse for the pastors and preachers, whose job it is to teach from the Bible. Their congregations have grown up being told that the soul lives after the body dies…just like you have. The idea of a separate soul is one of the ideas the Hebrews picked up from the pagan nations in which they lived for so many years and from the Greeks who dominated them for so long…ideas that God says are wrong. That's why I gave you your Bible, Breanna. I hope you will always search out the truth for yourself."

"Oh, I will, Gammy!"

"Then remember that Ecclesiastes 7:14 explains that 'man shall know nothing after he is gone'."

"WOW!"

"Here, look up soul," her grandmother instructed, handing her the encyclopedia, already opened at the proper page.

"Do you want me to read it?"

"Please." She could barely keep from smiling at the young girl's apparent interest. What if it was past her bedtime…these were important things for her to learn. Breanna began to read,"*Among Old Testament Isra…*"

"Israelites" her grandmother prompted.

"*'Israelites and New Testament Christians, the human being was considered to be an organis…mic?*"

"Yes, organismic. That's a functioning whole. All one."

"'*...organismic unit so that the Hebrew word 'nefesh',*'" (She looked up to make sure she had pronounced it correctly. She had.) "'*...and the Greek soul referred to the functioning unit of an individual rather than some part of him'.*" She looked at her grandmother, smiled, and added her own two cents' worth. "Hey. It says the soul's not just a part of a person."

"Keep reading. You'll find that it says it even more clearly."

"'*In other words,*'" she read, "'*the soul was the living mortal person and not a homesick visitor from the eternal region.*'" She giggled, then continued, "'*and there was nothing about the living mortal person, in part or as a whole, which was expected to survive the death of the functioning organism.*'" She emphasized organism to point out that she remembered.

"Now, in your own words."

"The soul is the person. You know, like Adam was after God breathed life into him. Part of us doesn't die and leave another part alive."

"So a soul is a complete, living person?"

"It does say that, doesn't it?"

"Yes, Honey. Soul and person can generally be used interchangeably. Anytime you see the word soul in the Bible, you'll find that it means person, people, life, I, me, they, anyone, everyone...heart, sometimes 'mind', or anything that pertains to a living creature. For instance, Acts 3 verse 23, uses three different words depending on the translation you have. In yours, the New King James Version, translated from the Greek language, it says, '*every soul*'. In mine, which was translated from Aramaic—the language Jesus spoke—the same verse, says, *'every person'*. But in the New International Version, it just says, *'anyone'*, but they all mean the same thing."

"Gee!"

"In Romans 13, verse 1 it says, *'Let every soul be subject to the governing authority'*. That is telling every one to be subject to the government. That has to mean the whole person...a living person...don't you think?"

"Sure!"

"And in Ephesians 5, verse 19, your Bible says, *'speaking to one another'* while mine reads, *'speaking to your souls'*. The word soul is used in the Bible over five hundred and twenty-five times.

"I did a study of the word, using six different translations of the Old and New Testaments and an additional seventh translation of the New Testament. It's probably a little too much for you right now, but I'll give it to you, and in years to come, you may enjoy studying it." (Attached as Addendum A)

"Why didn't they just use the right word so we can understand it?"

Her grandmother couldn't help but laugh. "Well, Sweetie, they did. It's just that man has changed the meaning to suit the things he wants to believe."

"Gammy, what about the people who are suppose to be able to talk to the dead... talk to people who have messages for their folks who are still alive?"

Her grandmother threw her head back and laughed aloud. "I'll bet you think that the Bible doesn't say anything about such a thing, don't you?"

Breanna smiled sheepishly.

"Well, Isaiah, chapter 8, verse 19 tells us that those who inquire of the dead concerning the living are not of God."

"Is there anything that the Bible doesn't talk about?"

"Not much," her grandmother responded laughingly.

Breanna pondered that for a moment, then, as though her mind had been invaded by another thought, she spoke. "So if Jesus is going to raise us from the dead, we can't be up in heaven when He comes."

"Exactly. Daniel, who was one of God's greatest prophets, tells us that we shall rest...which, in the Bible, means sleep in death...until the end of the days. Do you know what the end of the days means?"

"Isn't that when Jesus comes back?" She seemed to be taking that in before she continued. "But Gammy, isn't Daniel in the Old Testament? Jesus wasn't even born then, so how did Daniel know?"

"Because God told him. But it's also in the New Testament. First Corinthians 15, verses 52 and 53 tell us that we will be raised at the last days. Acts 17:31" she continued, "tells us that God has appointed a day when Jesus, as His agent, will judge the world. If we believe that the soul is some immortal part of the body that flies off at death, then when is the judgment?...and why? The Bible tells us...many times...that all believers will be judged at the same time. If there were a separate soul that goes off to heaven when we die, when was it judged righteous so as to be able to enter the heavenly Kingdom?"

Breanna was silent, so her grandmother continued. "When

you are thinking about this and when others question you about this belief, you should know that there are plenty of other verses that tell you the same thing. There is Psalms 6, verse 5 that says, '*In the grave there is no remembrance*'. Ecclesiasates, chapter 3 verses 19 and 20 explain that when we die, we turn to dust...and that there is no difference in humans and animals after death."

Breanna seemed transfixed. "When will the judgment be, Gammy?"

"We don't know, but Jesus told us that we should be always ready because when he comes, it will be a sudden surprise... without warning.
If King David, whom the Bible tells us in Acts 13:22, was '*a man after God's own heart*' and was '*dead and buried and not assigned into the heavens*', is it likely that any other of the faithful would be assigned to the heavens either?"

"Does the Bible tell us King David's not in heaven?"

"Yes, in Acts again, chapter 2, verses 29 and 34. Daniel was told, too, in Daniel 12:13, to '*rest till the end*' and that he would '*arise*' at his '*appointed time, at the end of the days.*'"

After thinking about that a minute, Breanna spoke again. "What does the Bible mean when it says that if I'm absent from my body, I'm present with the Lord? Doesn't absent from the body mean dead? And if I'm present with the Lord, doesn't that mean I'm in heaven?"

"Well, Honey, we ought to search that out, but I think its your sleepy time. Tomorrow is Saturday. Why don't we work on that one in the morning?"

"O.K!" she exclaimed, scooched down under the covers

and gave a big smile as she got her second good night kiss.

"Breanna, let me give you one more thing to think about. When Jesus died on the cross, did He have some part of Him that left and went to heaven? No! He remained asleep in the grave until God resurrected Him. If Jesus had to wait to be resurrected, don't you think we will certainly have to wait, too?"

"I hadn't thought about that. Gammy." she continued as her grandmother was about to close her door, "did Jesus live in heaven with God before he came to earth?"

"Not according to the Bible." She came in and again sat on the edge of Breanna's bed. She was going to have a hard time getting away from the girl's questions, but was delighted that she had such an interest in her Bible. How great it would be if all young people were as interested.

"Then who was God talking about when he said, 'Let us make man in our own image?' Who was the *us* and the *our*?"

"While chapter 1, verse 26 of Genesis says that God made man like 'us', in 'our' image, the Scripture isn't specific as to whom He is referring. However, I believe that God was talking about the angels that dwelt...and dwell...with Him in heaven. You remember that angels were mistaken for men throughout the Scriptures. In Genesis 18, when three messengers of God...angels...came to Abraham, they came as men. When the angels came to Lot in Genesis 19, he mistook them for men."

"I remember reading those stories, but I didn't really think about them being men like Adam."

"Jesus warned the Disciples and the Apostles not to forget to entertain strangers because they might be entertaining *angels unaware. "*

"Where is that in the Bible?"

"Hebrews, chapter 13, verse 2. And Breanna, we're told in Luke 20, verse 36, that when we are resurrected, we will be like the angels."

"Where did the angels come from, Gammy?"

"We don't know that. The Bible doesn't tell us that. I have my own idea, but it is only speculation, based on what I *do* know."

"Where do you think they came from?"

"My own suspicion is that the heavenly angels are the saints of a former creation...an earlier universe...and are those who received their salvation in whatever way God set up for them in that time and place. We just don't know. We only know that they, too, are children of God."

"Just like we will be children of God," Breanna added excitedly. Then she frowned. "But how do we get to be children of God?"

"By becoming brothers and sisters of Christ. This we do by learning all about Him, accepting Him as our Savior, being baptized into Him, and living our lives, as nearly as we can, like He lived His."

"Then I'll be God's daughter? Wow!"

"Now, back to your question about whether Jesus lived in heaven with God before he was born. Those who believe that He did, quote Revelations 22:13 as proof. That verse tells us that Jesus is the *'Alpha and Omega, the Beginning and the End, the First and the Last'*. This, they insist, means that Jesus was God the Son and was with God, the Father from the beginning of time and would be till the end. But rather than proving that Jesus was with His Father from the beginning, it proves that He was not. God had no beginning and will have no end, but was and is eternal."

"What does eternal mean, Gammy?"

"Just that. That He had no beginning…that He has always been, and that He will have no ending…but always will be."

"Then what does it mean when it says Jesus is the First and the Last…the Beginning and the End?"

"That verse in Revelation does not speak of the same beginning as the beginning of the universe described in Genesis. In the Revelation verse, Jesus Himself is speaking, and He is speaking of the beginning of the church…the creation of new men and women. In the New Testament, the words create  or creation  are often used to mean regeneration."

"Regeneration?"

"Yes, it means to make new. There are many Scriptures that make that clear. In Ephesians 2, verse 10, we are told that the disciples are created in Chist; in Galations 6, verse 15, that if we are in Christ, we become a new creation. The same thing is said in 2 Corinthians 5, verse 17. In Christ, we are new creations. Before Jesus was born, God revealed that He would be born. He said, '*I will be to Him a Father and He shall be to Me a Son*'. If Jesus had already been in existence with God in heaven, instead of I *will be* His Father and He *shall be* My Son', wouldn't God have said, 'I *am* His Father and He *is* My Son'?"

"Oh, yeah. So He's talking about Jesus becoming His Son after Jesus is born!"

"Sure. These were prophesies of things that were to

happen in the future, and the relationship between God and Jesus was also to be a future relationship as Father and Son. One more thing I'd like you to be aware of before you run into it when you discuss this subject with others. People who advocate this theory that Jesus lived before he was born will point to John 1, verses 1 through 3. This Scripture says that, '*In the beginning was the word, and the word was with God and the word was God*'. Word is translated from logos and logos does mean word . However, where the church goes wrong on this subject is their definition of logos. They insist that it means Jesus and therefore, the Scripture says that Jesus was in the beginning with God and that He is God.

"But if you study the word logos from sources other than theologians, you will find that it only took on the meaning Jesus after the church developed the doctrine of an eternal Jesus. Until that time, it meant, for the most part, God's plan.

"There is no doubt that God's plan was with Him from the beginning, and that Jesus was to be a part of that plan. But that does not, in any way, mean that logos means Jesus. Do you understand, Breanna?"

"I think so, Gammy. I'll study it some more and if I have trouble, I'll ask you."

"Now, young lady," she said, looking at her watch, "you'd better get to sleep before your mother comes and spanks us both. While you're getting to sleep, I'll be downstairs listing some more verses for you that will show you that Jesus only came into being when he was born as a flesh and blood…mortal…person."

"O K, Gammy. Just one more question. Is Jesus God?"

"Whoooo! You're giving me too many questions at once.

Tomorrow we'll finish up on what 'absent from the body' means, and I'll put 'is Jesus God?' on the list of subjects to cover later. Whether Jesus is God will take a lot of time because it is the most important thing you will ever need to know and I want you to be sure to understand it."

"OK, Gammy. I love you."

"And I love you…more than you know. Good night, Sweetie."

Another kiss.

* * *

Settled at the dining room table after everyone else was in bed, Gammy decided to write a paper on the subject of an eternal Jesus…or proof that no such Jesus existed…so that Breanna could have it to study and to keep.

She started with John 3 verse 16, a verse that almost everyone who has been near a Christian church has heard and most know by heart.

She began to type:

*"For God so   loved the world that He gave his only begotten Son so that who ever believes in Him should not perish, but have everlasting life."*

Breanna, the first word I want you to focus on in this verse is the word 'begotten'. While I want you to look up the word yourself, I'm going to put the meaning here so that this paper will be complete for any use you might want to make of it later. A begotten son, or to beget a son, means that the father created the child by making a woman pregnant.

In the case of Jesus, Mary was made pregnant by the power of God (Luke 1, verse 35), and gave birth to Jesus, just as any mother would have a baby.

And just as you inherited your mom's good nature and your dad's desire to learn, Jesus inherited characteristics of both His mother and His Father.

From His human mother, he derived the sinful nature common to all mankind, as we are told in Romans 8, verse 3, including the ability to be tempted as any other man, thus the ability to sin. (Hebrews 4, verse 15)

From His Father, God, He inherited latent spiritual tendencies that strengthened Him to conquer that sinful nature…and therefore to develop divine characteristics. (1 John 3, verse 9)

Breanna, to believe that Jesus was with God before creation, and that He was the man after which Adam was patterned, we must stretch our imaginations and believe more.

We would need to believe that He, Jesus, was a grown man when He was with God in heaven before His birth, as the pattern for the grown man, Adam; We would need to believe that when it came time for Jesus to come to earth, He had to be reduced from that grown man to a sperm…God's seed…that was to be in Him (1John 3, verse 9) and that was to cause Mary's pregnancy. (Luke 1, verse 31);

Then, as a Trinitarian, believing that the Holy Ghost is a separate person of the One God, i.e., God the Holy Ghost; and that He (God the Holy Ghost) came upon Mary, impregnating her with that seed that grew into Jesus, you'd need to believe that Jesus was the son of God the Holy Ghost rather than the son of God the Father . The Scriptures say, "the Holy Ghost shall come upon thee (Mary)' (Luke 1, verse 35)...thou shall conceive in thy womb and bring forth a son, and shall call his name Jesus" (Luke 1, verse 31).

We would have to believe that the conception therefrom resulted in a full-term baby which was born flesh and blood (John 1, verse 14, and Chapter 3, verse 6); and then, that this baby grew to be a man again. (1 Corinthians 15, verse 21 and 1st Timothy 2, verse 5).

How simple was the True doctrine, that through the Power of God, Mary became pregnant with God's Son. God said Jesus was His Son! Jesus said He was God's Son! Why can't we believe them? Until after Jesus' birth, God was never referred to as Father. Though He had been the Father of His created son, Adam, God had not "fathered" a child before Christ, and was never called Father during the centuries covered by the Old Testament.

Words such as birth and conceive and begotten, (Matthew 1, verses 18 and 20; Luke 1, verse 35) used to describe Christ's arrival, preclude the possibility of a prior existence, but *scream* of the beginning of existence.

My dearest Breanna, please study these passages so that you will understand not only when Jesus came into existence, but who He really is. It's the most important thing for you to ever know.

She folded the papers, put them by Breanna's place at the table and went off to enjoy a good night's sleep.

# Chapter 2
## Doesn't The Bible Say Jesus Came Down? *and* Will We Spend Eternity In Heaven?

Gammy had just settled down to a cup of hot tea when she could hear Breanna running down the stairs. The girl appeared in the sun-lighted kitchen, wearing blue jeans, a pink blouse and clutching her Bible to her chest.

"Hi, Sweetie, want some hot chocolate?"

"Mmmmm." A broad grin crossed her face and her head bobbed up and down on her pretty neck like one of the bobble-headed dolls often seen in the rear window of vehicles. She laid her Bible on the table and pulled up a chair for herself. Her grandmother stirred the chocolate syrup into the microwave-heated milk, reminding Breanna of when she had been a small girl and spent time with her grandmother during summer vacations. She still felt like a little girl around her grandmother... and she liked it.

"Here we are," Gammy said as she sat the mug down in front of the smiling youngster.

"Thank you, Gammy," and she began blowing across the cup to cool its contents.

"What gets you up so early on Saturday morning?" was the teasing question.

"Gammy! You know! You said we could talk about being absent from the body."

Her grandmother had to laugh. "Oh, is that right?" she chided. They both laughed. "How about first looking over the verses I found to show you that Jesus wasn't in existence until He was born as a baby. See if you have any questions about that, then we'll go to the subject of absent from the body."

Breanna opened the paper she'd been fingering and began to read. She obviously was rereading several of the passages, but there were no questions forthcoming. When she had completed all the pages, she laid it aside, looked seriously at her grandmother, and posed a question. "But doesn't the Bible say that Jesus came down from heaven?"

"Where, in the Bible, did you see that?"

"I don't think I know, I just know that's what they teach in Sunday School." She wasn't surprised at the good-natured scolding contained in her grandmother's look.

"Well, how about if I give you a little project? I'd like you to make me a list of the places in your Bible that say Jesus came down from heaven. I'll give you a hint. I think you'll find them in the Gospel of John."

"OK. How about if I do that like homework…tonight after dinner?" she asked. However, knowing that her grandmother had already told her that Jesus wasn't with God before He was born, she wondered if she'd find the passages she'd be searching for.

"Now, to the subject at hand," her grandmother began as she cleared her tea cup from the table, "what does Paul mean when he says 'absent from the body' and 'present with the

Lord'?" Opening Breanna's Bible, she continued. "Here we are. Let's start with Second Corinthians, chapter 5, verse 6. You drink your cocoa and I'll read it to you."

"O K."

"'*As long as we are at home in the body, we are absent from our Lord.*' Honey, all through the Bible the phrases '*in the body*','*in the flesh*','*in the world*' or '*of the world*', are used to describe our sinful, human natures. Here, Paul is saying that if we are at home, if we are comfortable, in those sinful natures, we cannot be doing the things our Lord would have us do. He goes on, in verse 8, to say, *'that is why we are confident and anxious to be absent from the body and present with our Lord.'*

"Paul, with his love of the Gospel and whose life was devoted to teaching that Gospel of God's Kingdom and of Jesus Christ, would never say that he was anxious to die…only that he was anxious to be absent from the sinful nature with which he, and all of us, are born. His expression of wanting to be present with the Lord meant only that he wanted to be more like Jesus in his life."

Breanna sat motionless and speechless, absorbing every word her grandmother spoke.

"Preachers in almost all denominations stand in front of their congregations, saying'*absent from the body*', throwing their arms toward heaven screaming, '*present with the Lord*,' and telling their congregations that it means that the instant they die they will be with God in heaven."

"And that's not what it means?"

"Paul, in this letter to the Corinthians, is teaching the same lesson of change that he has been expounding since his conversion. No one could be more qualified to teach such a lesson than Paul. He persecuted the Believers to the point of capturing and sending them to their deaths…until Jesus appeared to him and made a Believer of him. Paul knew more about changing from sin to righteousness than even those chosen by Jesus to be His Apostles. This was the lesson Paul taught throughout his teaching years.

"In his letter to the Romans, in chapter 6, verses 11 through 13, Paul uses different words, but the message is the same. He explains that when Believers are baptized into Jesus Christ, the sinful body is destroyed…is dead; and such baptized Believers should no longer serve sin…that is, should be absent from the body…away from their sinful, natural, worldly selves. He explains that we must consider ourselves 'dead *to* sin' but 'alive *from* sin' through Jesus Christ. In other words, having '*put off sin*', we are '*present with the Lord*'."

"In other words," Breanna volunteered, "absent from the body doesn't mean really dead, it just means dead to sin?"

"That's exactly what he means. It means that if we are happy with our sinful selves, we are separated from God. If we are happy with the way we are, we don't spend time trying to be more like Jesus, as God wants us to."

"Oh, yeah!" Breanna was excited at her sudden understanding.

"Is Paul telling them that if they die they will be with God?" Before Breanna could answer, her grandmother continued. "In Romans 8:10, Paul tells them clearly what he means. …'*if Christ is in you, the body is dead because of sin, but the spirit is life because of righteousness*.' That is the death and life Paul teaches. Death of the old life by baptism, resulting in a new life 'with the Lord'… a new life on earth…not in heaven."

Breanna was fascinated.

"You see," her grandmother continued, "absent from the body simply means the putting aside of our sinful tendencies and being present with the lord describes the new life of those who have been born again through baptism into Jesus Christ."

"Don't the preachers know this, Gammy?"

"Well, if Paul had known that the ministers and teachers were going to teach only from 2 Corinthians 5: 6 and 8, and were going to ignore all the other teachings on the subject, I'm sure he would have inserted parenthetical explanations, such as: 'As long as we are at home (content and satisfied) in the body (in our sinful natures) we are absent from our Lord (we are not spiritual in our worship)…This is why we are confident and anxious to be absent from the body (anxious to overcome our natural, sinful natures) and be present with our Lord (to be more spiritual in our lives.)'."

"That might have been a good idea." Breanna laughed.

"But Paul knew that God had instructed Believers to consider all of the Scriptures together; had commanded them to search to see if what they heard was true."

"Why don't people do that?"

"Gee, Honey, I guess they're just too lazy. They find it easier to listen to what their pastors or priests tells them and accept it as true. That's what the Bible warned us would happen. For instance, the idea of an immortal soul appeals to people, and people tend to believe what they want to believe.

It's too bad, too, because if you believe a lie, you will end up eternally separated from God. You won't get to see that wonderful Kingdom He's preparing for us. Our only hope is to learn, while we are alive, what the Truth is; to live in it, and to teach it to others so that when Christ returns we will be able to receive the immortal life that is promised to those who believe in Truth."

"Gammy, I really want to learn the Truth," Breanna said earnestly.

"And I want you to. Either we accept the teachings of the Bible, or we don't. If we don't, then we shouldn't call ourselves Christians, for the very foundation of Christianity is supposed to be the Bible."

"I'll try to learn the Truth, Gammy. Thank you so much for my Bible...but why do the churches teach that people go to heaven when they die?"

"It's just one of the pagan beliefs...the beliefs of the idol worshipers...beliefs later introduced into the Christian churches a couple of hundred years after Jesus died. I guess they thought it would be comforting to people who lost loved ones to believe that they were somehow still around."

"But didn't Jesus tell the sinner that died on the cross next to him that he would be with him in heaven that day?" That was one of the stories she had gotten from Sunday School class.

"That's an example of what I was telling you about interpretations being influenced by the beliefs we already have. It also shows the danger in not considering other Scriptures. Let's look at the verse. You'll find it in Luke chapter 23 verse 43.'

She could have found it more quickly herself, but she let Breanna search it out. Again, she was surprised at how quickly she began to read.

"*'Jesus said to him, truly I say to you, today you will be with me in Paradise.'* Doesn't that say he will go to heaven that day?"

"Now go back and read verse 42. This is where the sinner being crucified with Jesus asks Jesus to remember him."

"*'And he said to Jesus, remember me, my Lord, when you come in your kingdom.'*"

"That tells us what?"

"That he wanted Jesus to remember him?"

"When did he want Him to remember him?"
"When Jesus sets up His kingdom."

Her grandmother reached and took a note pad and pencil from beside the phone. On it, she printed:

TRULYISAYTOYOUTODAYYOUWILLBEWITHMEINPARADISE

"Read that to me, Breanna."

Breanna took the scrap of paper, but couldn't make heads nor tails of it.

"That is the way the original Scriptures were written. All capital letters and no punctuation. When the translators got hold of it, they put in the comma where they thought it ought to be, making it appear that Jesus was telling the thief that he would go to His Kingdom that day."

"He wasn't?"

"Jesus was telling him that He could *tell* him today, right that minute, that when He set up His Kingdom, he would be with Him. He would not have to wait till the Kingdom was set up to know. In other words, if you move the comma and put it after today, instead of before today, it reads entirely differently. The translators added the punctuation according to what they already believed."

"How do you know which is right?"

"Because we look at more than just that one verse. For one thing, Jesus couldn't have meant that he would be with Him in paradise today because Jesus, Himself, wasn't in paradise today and He knew that He wasn't going to be in paradise today. He knew He would be in the tomb for three days. As a matter of fact, He was on earth forty days after His resurrection before He went to God's house in heaven."

"Oh, that's right. So He's just *telling* him today that he will be there when Jesus sets up His Kingdom."

"That's right. And when did Jesus set up His Kingdom?"

Breanna stared, blankly, at her grandmother.

"It has now been more than two thousand years since that day, and Jesus still has not come to set up God's Kingdom on earth."

"So Jesus hadn't set up any Kingdom that the thief could go to that day?"

"You're a much better analyst than many adults, Breanna. I hope you will always search the Scriptures to learn the Truth, Honey, and not just accept what others tell you...not even what I tell you...and certainly not what preachers tell you from their pulpits."

Breanna threw her arms around her grandmother's neck and assured her that she would search out answers for herself.

"Your Bible doesn't do it, but in mine, there is a footnote that says, '*Ancient texts were not punctuated. The comma could come before or after today*'. Go back now and read Jesus' answer, putting the comma after the word today. '*Truly I say to you today, you will be with me in Paradise.*'" If you think about the fact that it couldn't mean they would *be there* today, the comma can only be in one place...*after today*."

"Yeah! We know that this criminal died, so was there a part of him that flew off to be with the Lord?"

"Nope!"

"When Paul wrote to those Believers in Corinth, he was telling them that there are only two states in which, as living beings, they can exist. One, in the body …their sinful bodies. The other is their spiritual bodies…when they are living, as nearly as they can, the type of life that Jesus lived...then they are present with the Lord. We have mortal bodies which can die. We will, when Jesus returns and raises us from the dead, be given immortal bodies, which will never die, only if we worship in *TRUTH* and are baptized into Jesus Christ."

"So when we die, we just stay dead till He comes?"

This seemed unbelievable to the child who had been taught most of her young life that, if she was good, she would fly off to heaven at death and would spend eternity in heaven with Jesus.

"Yes, we do, Sweetheart, just as though we were sleeping. There is no intermediate state."

"What does intermediate mean?"

"In-between. In the Scriptures there's no indication of a life of any kind between the time we die and the time Christ raises us. Honey, look up Ecclesiastes, chapter 12, verse 7. Do you know where that is?"

"Sure!" And she quickly found the passage."

"What does it tell you?"

She read quietly to herself, then looked unbelievingly into her grandmothers eyes. "It says," and she dropped her eyes to the page, *'when we die, we turn to dust and our spirit returns to God?'"*

"Read it again. Whose spirit returns to God?"

"Oh, *the* spirit."

"And whose spirit was it that gave Adam life?"

"God's."

"So when God takes back his spirit, there is no life left. Only the dust from which we are made, right?"

"Oh, yeah!"

"Now, let's turn to Job." When they both had found the book, her grandmother spoke again. "Go to chapter 34 and let's read verses 14 and 15."

"*'If He'*...and who is He?"

"God!"

"Yes. *'If God should gather to Himself His spirit'*...now that tells us again whose spirit we're talking about...*'all flesh would perish together, and man would return to dust'*...again, God's spirit, not ours."

"Then there's nothing left of a person who dies?"

"To die is to reverse the process used to create Adam. God's spirit...or breath...gave Adam life. When God removes that spirit...or takes away man's breath...man dies. For the one who dies, it's like a deep sleep. Psalms 146, verse 4 tells us that we return to the earth and our plans and thoughts perish.

"We don't know anything?" This seemed hard for her to absorb.

"We don't know anything! It tells us that very thing in Ecclesiastes 9:5, if you'd like to look it up."

"I believe it if you tell me its there."

By this time, Gammy had found the verse and read it aloud. *"'For the living know that they will die but the dead know nothing'."*

"Then Grandpa isn't in heaven watching over us." She seemed sad at the thought.

"Honey, there are two places in the Bible that tells us specifically that he isn't. Job 14 verses 19 through 21, tell us that after we are dead, our loved ones can get lots of honors and we don't know anything about it...or they can be dishonored, and we don't know that either.

"Ecclesastes 7:14 says that man knows nothing after he is gone. I think it's pretty clear that Grandpa won't know anything until Jesus comes again."

"I think so, too, Gammy. We can see Grandpa after Jesus comes. He really has to wait a long time, doesn't he?"

"Maybe, but Grandpa won't realize it. When you go to bed at night and toddle off to sleep, what is the next thing you remember?"

"When Daddy wakes me in the morning?"

"And, without looking at the clock, do you have any idea how long you've been sleeping?"

"No," and suddenly she understood. "So that's what it's like?"

"It is! *IF* you have worshiped Him in Truth, Jesus will wake you and you will not have any idea how long you had been waiting. In fact, it will be so wonderful, you won't even *care* how long it was."

Breanna grinned from ear to ear. "I have to go tell my friend," she squealed. "I bet she doesn't know." She disappeared through the French door, into the sunlight, clutching her Bible as she ran.

* * *

After dinner that night, Breanna took her Bible and her grandmother's Concordance and headed for her room to look for the verses that told her that Jesus came down from heaven. She was busy for over two hours before she called her grandmother to come kiss her good night.

"Well, did you finish your project?"

"Yep!" She handed her grandmother the sheet of lined yellow paper on which she had typed her assignment of Scriptural verses and their references.

"Well, let's see what we have here." She took the paper from Breanna and noted how neatly she had prepared it.

> Jesus Came Down From Heaven
> By Breanna
>
> John 3 verse 13 says: "no man hath ascended upto heaven but he that came down from heaven, even the son of man which is in heaven." (Jesus speaking)
>
> John 3 verse 31: says, "He who comes from above

is above all."

John 3 verses 34: In this one, Jesus is the one God sent.

John 6 verse 38: Jesus said: "I have come down from heaven."

John 6 verse 51: says, "I am the living bread which came down from heaven." (that's Jesus, too.)

John 6 verse 58: Jesus says "This is the bread which came down from heaven." (Talking about himself).

John 6 verse 62: says, "ye shall see the son of man ascend up where he was before..." Jesus saying he is going to heaven where he was before.

John 8 verse 23: Jesus says, "Ye are from beneath; I am from above."

Her grandmother looked at Breanna and complimented her on the paper.

"You were right," Breanna said, "they were all in John."

She took Breanna's Bible and turned to the Gospel of John. "Here, in John 3:13," her grandmother read, "John says, *'No man hath ascended up to heaven but He that came down from heaven, even the Son of Man which is in heaven'.* Followed in John 6:33 by *'the bread of God is He which cometh down from heaven'* and verse 38 in that same 6th chapter, which quotes Jesus as saying, *'For I have come down from heaven'."*

"Doesn't that tell us that Jesus came down from heven…and if He came down from heaven, didn't He have to be there with God in order to do that?"

"John's gospel passages often employed the Old Testament language of theophany."

"What does that mean?"

"It means that the manifestation of divine power is referred to as *'God coming down'* and the completion of the theophany is God going up or ascending. For an example of the use of theophany, let's look at Genesis 11 verse 5, wherein God is said to have come down to see the tower at Shinar, which later became known as the Tower of Babel."

"That's where the word babbling came from, isn't it?"

"I expect it did. God *'scattered them abroad and confounded their language'* so that they couldn't continue with the building of the tower, which they were trying to build to reach to heaven. Can you imagine what it must have sounded like with all these people speaking in languages that were strange, not only to the others, but to themselves?"

Breanna laughed as she tried to picture the confusion that must have occurred.

"Since we know from 1st Timothy chapter 6 verse 16, that no one has ever seen God, we know that He did not, Himself, come down. He came down by His angels…His messengers…to manifest Himself…to accomplish His purposes through others. This was not an earthly appearing of God. He did not descend except by his angels, or by the use of his power."

Breanna was thinking about that, not sure she was convinced. "So God didn't come down?"

"If we take a look at Exodus 3 verse 8, God said, *'I am come down to deliver them out of the hands of the Egyptians'*. We all know the story of how Moses was sent to bring the Hebrews out of Egypt. God did not *'come down'* to do that job Himself. He came, manifested in the person of Moses, to accomplish His purpose of delivering His people."

Breanna did remember the story of Moses, and this now began to make sense to her.

"Exodus 19 verse 18 tells us that the Lord will *'come down'* in the sight of all the people upon Mt. Sinai…but then it goes on to explain that the Lord descended *'in the form of fire and smoke'* and an *'earthquake'*. So, you see, God can come down in any way He chooses, and He chooses to do so through His agents or His extraordinary power.

"Just as God did not come down, neither did Jesus come down. His origin was heavenly because God was His Father and His teachings were His Father's. We know that because Luke 1, verse 35 tells us so. Jesus taught *only* what His Father told Him. He said.*'I speak to the world those things which I have heard from my Father'*. That's found in John 7, verse 16, but we are reminded of that throughout the New Testament."

"Didn't I see that in John, too?"

"You did. John 8 verses 26 and 28."

"Then if He only says those things that He heard his Father say, didn't He have to be in heaven to hear them?"

"Breanna, Jesus learned the things that His Father wanted

Him to say and do by studying the Scriptures…just as you and I are directed to do. At the age of twelve, He was sitting in the Temple, asking and answering questions of the teachers. At that early age He was already amazing the teachers with His wisdom."

"Was that in John, too?"

"That's from Luke 2 verses 46 and 47. And if you go on to verse 49, you'll see that He said, *'I am about my Father's business'*. Surely we can't believe that he was in the temple learning carpentry…the business of his earthly father, Joseph? He was about His heavenly Father's business in his heavenly Father's house…the Temple, learning what His Father wanted Him to teach."

"You mean Jesus learned about God from the Bible?"

"Well, the Bible, as such, wasn't available at that time. The Old Testament Scriptures were written on Scrolls. And it wasn't until many years after Jesus' death, that the Bible was assembled…when Old and New Testaments were brought together. Jesus learned, from the Scriptures, about Himself; about the circumstances of His birth; about His purpose in the world; about His pending death; and about His ultimate resurrection."

"Then He didn't get actual instructions from God in heaven?"

"No, He found all of his instructions in the Holy Scriptures…the infallible Word of God. The same place you and I are suppose to go for our own instructions."

Breanna thought for a few minutes, then, as though her thoughts has skipped back to an earlier statement, she questioned her grandmother again. "How could the Old

Testament tell Him about Himself, since He hadn't even been born?"

"Oh, dear Breanna, that's the thing that makes us all wonder how the Jews could have missed the fact that Jesus was their Messiah! The Old Testament is so full of prophesies about Jesus…about how and where He'd be born…about what would happen to Him during His lifetime…how he would die…about his resurrection; and all of these things that were in the Old Testament came to pass just as they were written."

"Gammy, can you show me, in the Bible, where some of these things are?"

"Of course I will, Breanna. They are some of the most fascinating things about the Bible…the fact that for hundreds of years before He was born, God was telling His people that He was going to send His Son so that they could be saved by receiving Him…by believing in Him. And even though they were looking forward to that day, when it came, they missed it all together, because they were waiting for, and hoping for, a worldly king to lead them in battle against their enemies."

"When can we look those verses up, Gammy?"

"Well, how about right after lunch tomorrow? After church, I have something else I want to share with you."

"Great! But what else do you want to talk about?"

"We've talked about dying, but we haven't talked about heaven. How about if we check up on heaven after church tomorrow?"

"Sure."

She knelt and waited for her grandmother to join her in bedtime prayers, and this time she asked God to help her be more like Jesus. Afterwards she received her usual good night kiss, and was asleep almost before her grandmother could turn out the light.

* * *

Breanna had the homework the night before. it was now Gammy's turn to get to work. She had promised Breanna to show here where in the Old Testament there was information about the prophesies of Jesus' coming. She wanted to be prepared, so she took her Bible, her tablet and her pencil and settled under the best light in the living room.

# Chapter 3
# Worshiping With Nonbelievers

Breanna sat quietly with her mom, dad and grandmother in the fourth row pew of the family church. Well, it wasn't exactly the family church, as only Breanna attended regularly and then only for Sunday school. Gammy knew that her son and his wife were only there because of her visit. They both worked five to six days a week and the weekends were the only times they had to catch up on chores and shopping. But his mother was conscientious in attending her own church back home, so Greg and Michelle felt they needed to accompany her to services while she was with them.

The young minister spoke well and convincingly on the need for positive thinking though he never mentioned a Bible verse. The music was lively and the church was filled with young people…young married couples and teenagers. Certainly a good sign if they receive the True gospel, but on this particular day, there was no sign of that. The pastor did say that we should all live our lives as much like Jesus led His as we possibly can, which brought a reaction from Breanna. She looked up at her grandmother and smiled as if to say, "I knew that." Gammy returned the smile and patted her on the knee.

When communion was passed, Grammy did not participate and from the questioning look she received from Breanna, she knew she would have to answer questions about that…and she was happy that she would be able to explain it to her.

After the service, everyone shook hands with the minister as they left the church, and chatted with friends and acquaintances as they headed for their individual homes.

Almost before they were out of earshot of the pastor, the expected question came. "Gammy, why didn't you take communion?"

"Because I don't have the same beliefs as the members of that church. Actually, I don't believe they worship in Truth, and the Bible tells us not to fellowship with those who do not believe the Truth."

"If you don't believe the same thing, you can't take communion together?" This astounded Breanna. She'd never heard such a thing.

"Officially, nearly all so-called Christian denominations have rules against such togetherness-worship…but most of them ignore the rules. For the most part, members of their congregations don't even know what the rules are. In fact, I doubt that five percent of all church members even know what their church's beliefs are."

"Really?"…but it was more an exclamation than a question.

They piled into the car and headed home, each silent in his and her own thoughts.

On arrival, Michelle reminded Breanna to change her

clothes and she scurried off to obey. The rest of the family changed, too.

While Michelle prepared lunch, Greg repaired a leaking hose. Gammy sat in the living room with her Bible, waiting for Breanna to pounce on her. It wasn't long.

"Gammy, before we talk about heaven, will you explain to me again why you can't take communion at my church? I don't understand it."

"To 'fellowship' with others is often, in the Bible, referring to the breaking of bread, which you call communion. The Bible tells us, clearly, not to fellowship with unbelievers."

"What makes someone an unbeliever if they are members of a church and have been baptized?"

"An unbeliever is one who does not believe in the Jesus that the Apostles taught. To believe in a different Jesus is to know nothing."

"The Bible says that?"

"It does. Look at 1 Timothy, chapter 6, verses 3 and 4. Then, in verse 5 it tells you to keep away from people who are cut off from the Truth. Breanna, there can only be one Truth…if you don't know and believe *that* Truth, you should not be called a Christian."

"I guess I understand, but I had never heard it before. Will you tell me about heaven now?"

"Not till you students have had lunch," came Michelle's voice from the kitchen.

"You said we'd talk about heaven after lunch, so guess that's when we'll do it." Breanna laughed.

They left their Bibles on the dining room table and headed for the breakfast nook.

# Chapter 4
# Heaven: Our Eternal Home?

After lunch, Micah insisted on cleaning up the kitchen herself so that they could get back to their studies.

"Thanks, Mom. OK, Gammy, I guess I'm ready to learn about heaven," Breanna said as they headed back to their Bibles.

"Do you remember your original question...the one that set us out on this study journey through the Bible?"

After a short, thoughtful delay, Breanna answered, "Will my soul go to heaven when I die?"

"Well, you now know that no part of you will go to heaven when you die. The question, then, is will you *ever* go to heaven?"

Breanna's mouth fell open in disbelief that there would be any question.

"Tell me everything you know about heaven," instructed her grandmother.

"It's God's home."

"Does anyone else live there?"

"Sure, Jesus and the angels...but Grandpa's not there."

"No, Grandpa's not there." She smiled. "It would be nice

to think that he could be there looking down on the granddaughter that he loved so much, but do you remember where he is?" She gave Breanna's hand an affectionate squeeze.

"He's still asleep in his grave."

"Yes, he's waiting for Christ's return. So what happens when Christ comes?"

"Jesus will take us to heaven to God's Kingdom...just like He will the criminal that died on the cross next to His."

"Where does it say that the Kingdom Jesus sets up will be in heaven?"

Breanna's eyes were wide and searching. "Won't it?"

"Where did you get the idea that it would be?"

"The preacher said so. He said if we believe in Jesus, we will spend eternity with Him in heaven."

"What did I tell you about taking someone else's word for things?"

"You told me to look it up in the Bible," she said, hanging her head as though she'd committed some terrible sin, "but how do I look it up?" Her grandmother smiled.

"I bought you a little present," Gammy smiled, reaching behind her chair and bringing forth a package that was unmistakably a book.

"What is it?" Breanna asked as she tore away the wrapping and held the book in her hands. "A Concordance," she exclaimed, delighted to have her very own. She had used her grandmother's, but Gammy's was much smaller than this one.

Her grandmother took the book and opened it. "We want to know about the Kingdom," she said, "so we look up the word kingdom…just like using a dictionary. Do you remember how you looked up passages that told you that Jesus came down? Every word in the Bible is listed here, and it shows you where to look for it in your Bible. Here, here's the word kingdom." She showed it to Breanna, who took the book in her own hands.

*"The beginning of his k was Babel."* She looked quizzically at her grandmother.

"Once you find the word you're looking for, a sentence or part of a sentence from the Scripture is given, and the initial of the word you're looking for appears instead of the word itself. It's just a way of saving space. So that reference really reads, *'the beginning of his kingdom was Babel'.*"

Breanna remembered that from having used the smaller version.

"That was the first time the word kingdom was mentioned in the Bible. Now follow the line over to the right side of the page and It tells you that the phrase is found in Genesis 10:10. As you get to know your Bible better, you will know that that refers to a worldly kingdom and not to God's eternal Kingdom. That's why they put part of the verse there, so you can tell if it's what you're looking for."

"Hey, that's pretty smart." She didn't want to let her grandmother know that she'd figured that out for herself when she was working on her paper. There was one thing she didn't understand, however. "Why are some of these in plain print and some of them in dark print?"

"The bold…the dark…are words that were spoken by Jesus, Himself."

"That's why they don't have any dark print on those in the

Old Testament," Breanna stated matter-of-factly. This little girl was becoming very comfortable in her Bible.

"You can see that there are dozens of places where the word kingdom is used in the Bible. Let's go to the New Testament ...and what's the first book of the New Testament?"

"Matthew!" she exclaimed quickly, as though she were afraid that her grandmother would tell her before she could demonstrate her knowledge.

"Look here in the column on the right hand side of the page, and you can find Matthew by just going down the line of Scriptures and finding the abbreviation, Mt. The books of the Bible...and then the chapters and verses in those books...are all listed in the order in which they appear in the Bible."

"Let me!" and she grabbed the book back. "Oh, here it is! *'for the k...for the kingdom of heaven is at hand'*. That says that the Kingdom is in heaven. Hey, it says it two times...and it says, *'for theirs is the kingdom of heaven'*. Its got a lot of places where it says that in Matthew."

The child was excited that she was finding so many different verses to prove that God's Kingdom was in heaven. She looked closely at the page, then up at her grandmother.

"OK, we know that God's Kingdom is in heaven *now*, so let's search out something that tells us what we want to know about where it will be when we're in it. Move around here so we can both see the page."

Breanna adjusted the Concordance and her grandmother ran her finger slowly down the Scripture column while the inquisitive youngster watched closely.

"Let's try Luke 11 verse 2. That's one you already know." She turned to the passage in Breanna's Bible and began to read. '*And He said to them,*' and who is He?

"Jesus?"

"Yes, Jesus. '*And He said to them, when you pray say: Our Father who art in heaven*'," and Breanna joined in and they read together, '*hallowed be Your name. Your Kingdom come. Your will be done on earth as it is in heaven.*'" Where does that say God's kingdom is?"

"In heaven. So we go to heaven, don't we?"

"What does Jesus tell us to pray for?"

Breanna looked down at the passage again. Somehow, she couldn't figure out the question.

"Doesn't He tell us to pray for God's Kingdom to come...and for His will to be done on earth, just as it is in heaven?"

"Yeah." But she was still thinking.

"Do you think Jesus would tell us to pray for something that would never be?"

"But the preacher says that our rewards are being stored up in heaven, so how can we get our rewards if we don't go to heaven?"

"Because the Bible also tells us that Jesus is going to bring the rewards with Him when He comes '*to give every man, according to his work*'."

"It does?"

"In the very last chapter of the Bible, Revelation chapter 22, at verse 12."

"So God's Kingdom is going to be on earth?" This idea still seemed to surprise the child. "Isn't Jesus going to rule in the Kingdom?"

"Yes, after he comes back to get us and make us immortal. Honey, you are still a little young to be able to understand Revelation, but that is the book that Jesus wrote by dictating it to John in a dream. In it, He has John warn all the churches that they are not teaching the Truth…or that they are not keeping faith in Jesus as they once did. And it also tells what will happen in the future. He showed John…in this dream…the new Jerusalem coming down from heaven. Isn't that what Jesus told us to pray for?"

"Uh huh." Breanna seemed almost under a spell.

"And in the first chapter of Acts, in the 9th verse, we're told how Jesus went up into heaven, and then, in verse 11, that He will come down again in the same way he left."

"And is that when we are raised up from being dead?"

"That's the time. If you are in Christ, you will receive immortality when He returns. If you have already died, you will be first, and then those who are still alive at the time of His return, will be given immortality next. That is explained in 1st Thessalonians, chapter 4, verses 16 and 17."

"What does 'in Christ' mean, Gammy?"

"It means that you know who Jesus is; that you believe that He is God's Son; that you understand that He died as a sacrifice for you just as we all will die; that He rose again from the dead so that we, too, can some day rise again and have eternal life in God's Kingdom. Once we know all of this… understand and believe it…we will be baptized in Jesus' name. If you truly believe this, it will change your life…which means you are born again to a new life, just as Paul taught. You will then be in Christ…a daughter of God…an adopted sister to Jesus...a seed of Abraham...a Jew in God's eyes."

"What do you mean by a seed of Abraham?"

"That means a descendant, Honey. God promised all the land to Abraham's descendants, and we can become descendants of Abraham by accepting Jesus as our Savior."

"Was Jesus a descendant of Abraham?"

"He certainly was. He was a physical descendant...the seed by whom all the earth will be blessed, as we're told in Genesis 22:18. Then when we go to the New Testament in Galatians 3:16 reminds us that it is seed, singular, not seeds, plural. That refers to Jesus. The very first chapter of the first Gospel...The very beginning of the New Testament...gives the genealogy of Jesus, from Abraham right through Jesus, Himself. Turn to Matthew chapter 1 and start at verse 1."

Breanna opened her Bible and studied this list of Jesus' ancestors from Abraham, leading to His step father who was a descendant of David, and to His mother, who also, was of the line of David.

"This is what God had promised," Gammy said. "In addition to being of the seed of Abraham, God told us that Jesus would be born of the descendants of King David...who, of course, was a descendant of Abraham."

"Will all these people be in the Kingdom?" she asked as she studied it.

"No, not all of them. They were not all as righteous as Abraham was, which you'll learn as you study your Bible more, but surely some will be there."

"Gammy, I have a couple of questions. Does the Old Testament really talk about Jesus, and what the Kingdom is going to be like?"

"Tonight, instead of a bedtime story, maybe we can talk a little about both of those subjects. Would you like that?"

"Oh, yes!"

"I think you'll be surprised at how much the Old Testament says about Jesus."

They had been studying all afternoon…from the time they finished lunch to the time Michelle called them to the light supper she had prepared. Breanna laid aside her book and headed for the dining room and her favorite fruit salad. She was sure that only her Mom could create such a dish, but she was also anxious to finish supper so she and Gammy could talk about the Kingdom and the Old Testament stories of Jesus.

# Chapter 5
# The Old Testament Jesus

Breanna didn't have to be told that it was time to get ready for bed. She was so looking forward to her talk with Gammy, that she announced her own bedtime earlier than usual. By the time she had gotten into her pajamas, brushed her teeth and said her prayers, her grandmother was smilingly waiting at her bedside. Breanna literally jumped into bed and propped herself against the headboard.

Gammy smiled and unfolded the paper that she had prepared the night before, and laid it between them. Breanna's eyes widened.

"Wow, Gammy, how did you find out all these things? Do you know the Bible by heart?"

When her grandmother had finished laughing at the question, she responded. "No, Honey. It might have taken you a longer time, but it would have been an easy thing for you to have done yourself. Your Bible is set up to make such searches easy. Hand me your Bible."

Breanna handed it over eagerly and her grandmother just opened it without choosing any particular subject. It happened that she turned to the 24th chapter of the book of

Matthew. Closing her eyes, she touched a verse. It turned out to be verse 38.

"Here it says, *'For as in the days before the flood, they were eating and drinking, marrying and giving in marriage, until the day that Noah entered the ark'*. Now look here in this center section for verse 38, and you see that it refers you to Genesis, chapter 6, verses 3 through 5. What do you think you will find when you go back to that Scripture?"

"Is it the story of Noah and the Ark?"

"Pretty close. It's describes how people were living in those days before the floods, and it was pretty clear that they weren't worshiping God. This little section in the center of each page can help you understand a lot of things about your Bible. It can give you meanings of words and it refers you to other portions of the Bible where the same situations are described. So you see, when you learn in the New Testament that Jesus rode a donkey into Jerusalem, the Bible will tell you where that same thing is given in the Old Testament."

"Gee, that really does make it easier, doesn't it?"

"Breanna, tell me all you know about Jesus... His birth, his life, and his death."

"Well, He was born in Bethlehem… and His mother was a virgin and God was His Father…and there was a star in the sky that shined to show the shepherds where He was…" she paused. "I guess that's about all I know about his birth. Then as he grew up, he did not sin and he taught all the people about God. He was crucified on a cross, died, and was brought back to life by God and went to heaven."

"That's a pretty good summary. I expect that you know

that the gospels…

"Matthew, Mark, Luke, and John," Breanna chimed in quickly.

"Yes, Matthew, Mark, Luke, and John all tell those stories of Jesus. However, all of those things were prophesied…were told…hundreds and hundreds of years before Jesus was ever born."

"They were?" Breanna seemed puzzled..

"These Scriptures are sometimes said to speak of the Old Testament Jesus, but actually, they are things that were told to the Jews so that they would be able to recognize their Messiah when He came."

"But they didn't, did they?"

"No, most did not, though we have to remember that all of the Apostles were Jews, so some of them did."

"Are those the Old Testament verses that talk about Jesus?" Breanna asked, pointing to the paper her grandmother had prepared.

"Yes, would you like to go over them a little?"

"Sure! Where does it say He will be born in Bethlehem?"

Her grandmother looked down the list and found the verse in which Breanna was interested. "Micah, chapter 5, verse 2…which was prophesied seven hundred years before Christ was born…says that even though Bethelem is a small town, the Ruler of Israel will come forth from there. But you know what? I think the most exciting Old Testament verse about Christ's birth comes from Isaiah, chapter 7, verse 14. See if you feel the same way."

Breanna opened her Bible and found Isaiah right away. "What chapter?"

"Seven...verse 14.      Breanna began to read aloud. *"'Behold, the virgin shall conceive and bear a Son, and shall call his name Immanuel.'* WOW! And that was how long before Jesus was born, Gammy?"

"Over seven hundred years, Honey."

"And does the Old Testament tell us about His crucifixion, too?"

"It does, indeed. In Zechariah 12 verse 10, *'the one whom they have pierced'* speaks of Jesus being nailed to the tree, and in Psalm 22, verse 16, also says that *'they pierced my hands and my feet'.* And this was a thousand years before Christ was even born."

Breanna stared at the verse in disbelief but said nothing. Her grandmother, continued.

"The Old Testament was even more specific on the crucifixion, too. It told, in advance, that Jesus would ride into Jerusalem on a donkey; that the Romans would take his clothes and gamble for them; that none of his bones would be broken; that he would be buried; that he would rise on the third day; and that he would go to heaven to be with His Father. All this was told to the Jews...any who would listen...hundreds of years before Jesus even came into the world."

Breanna was speechless...and was obviously over-whelmed.

"I have prepared this paper (Addendum B) for you to keep in your notebook," she said as she handed the paper to Breanna. "It gives you the various prophesies and where they appear in the Old Testament...then goes on to tell you where they are fullfilled in the New Testament. You will enjoy looking them up and seeing how exact God was when He gave these messages to His people. You may be able to find other verses that I haven't even listed."

Breanna took the papers and folded them gently, placing them in the back of her Bible for safekeeping.

"Have you had enough for one night? Shall we wait till morning to talk about God's Kingdom?"

"OK, maybe we'd better. I am getting a little sleepy."

Her grandmother took Breanna's Bible from her and placed it on the chest beside her bed. She gave her a kiss on the forehead, and, after Breanna had kissed her too, tiptoed out of the room. Breanna was asleep before her grandmother reached the first floor.

# Chapter 6
# God's Kingdom

"So, you want to know what God's Kingdom will be like?"

"Oh, yes, Gammy. I know I want to go there...don't you?"

"Breanna, I don't think there is anything that could be more wonderful than being in God's Kingdom. That's why it's so important for us to prepare for it...to be ready...so that we don't get left out, because when Jesus comes, it will be quickly."

"The Bible says that?"

"Yes, in Revelation 3, verse 11, it says, *'Behold I am coming quickly. Hold fast what you have, that no man may take your crown'.*" Her grandmother recited the verse before Breanna could find it, but the girl had a question.

"What does it mean to hold onto what we have so we don't lose our crown?"

This brought a smile to her grandmother's face. "Jesus was speaking to the churches and He wanted them to hold onto their faith...to hang onto the Truth...so that they would not lose the rewards.....the crowns...that he wanted to give to them. You know, don't you, that we who are in the

Kingdom will be crowned princes and priests? That we will help Jesus rule the world for a thousand years?"

"We will!" Her eyes were wide with excitement."

"Sure. Revelations 5 verse 10 assures us that Jesus will reign on his throne on the earth and that we shall reign with Him on earth. Again, He's telling us that the Kingdom will be on earth."

"Yeah, but why does everybody say that we will go to heaven? The pastor says that Jesus is in heaven preparing a place for us."

"Jesus *is* in heaven, and He *is* preparing a place for us. He's making the preparations in heaven, but that does not mean that the Kingdom will be there when we are finally in it."

"I see," Breanna said, but it was clear that she did not see.

"Honey, we have to remember that there are no contradictions in the Bible. When you find two verses that seem to tell you different things, you have to look at them carefully and see which one is told in clear language that can only mean one thing. If you read John 4 verse 3 quickly, you assume Jesus was preparing a place for us to *go to* in heaven. But that contradicts the scripture that says, clearly, *'we will reign on earth'*. That is pretty clear, isn't it? So we have to go back to John and see if there is any way that that could mean something we hadn't seen before. Knowing that we have been told in clear language that Jesus' kingdom will be on earth, we then can see that this verse tells us that the preparations for the earthly kingdom are being made in heaven. When we look at it that way, there is no contradiction. This is the way we reconcile the two. The message is clear.

"You'd think the preachers would know all that." Her

voice seemed not only sad, but somewhat angry.

"Many do, and some will admit that if they tried to preach anything other than the false doctrines that the theology schools teach them, they'd be out of a job. The Scriptures tell us that the Truth is to be taught willingly, but not for money. That isn't the way preachers and pastors of today preach. The bigger the church the more money the pastor gets. Do you know that some of the very large churches pay their pastors hundreds of thousands of dollars a year?"

"Don't all churches pay their preachers?"

"Almost all of them, Honey. But that doesn't make it right. They should be given food and shelter, but their preaching should be from the heart and with the reward of eternal life to come in the future...not dollars today."

"Does your pastor get paid?"

"No, Breanna. All the men in our congregation take turns giving the exhortation...that is what most churches call the sermon. They study the Bible constantly, and each Sunday, one of them speaks of what it says."

"But what do they live on?"

"They have other jobs. God provides them with all they need when they devote their lives to Him and His Son. In fact, some of them are quite wealthy. And if any members of our congregation have needs they cannot meet, the other members of the church...which we call the ecclesia, which is the name used in the days of the Apostles...then other members of the ecclesia will provide for them or help them, or take care of them, until they can get on their feet."

"You mean if a member of your church gets sick and doesn't have anyone to take care of them, another member will take care of them?"

"Another member...or several other members... or, if needed, the church will pay someone to come in and take care of them. When men preach for money, they miss so much of God's message. They preach what they think people want to hear rather than what is true. That's why I want you always to go to your Bible so that you don't miss the Truth."

"Oh, Gammy, you make me so happy." She jumped from beneath the covers and threw her arms around her grandmother's neck.

"I didn't do it, Honey. Jesus did it...but I'm glad it makes you happy. That makes *me* happy...and I think it makes Jesus happy, too. It's like the thief on the cross. You figured out which interpretation was correct by checking other Scriptures and finding that one of them couldn't possibly be correct. Jesus wasn't in Paradise that day....He wasn't going to be in paradise that day, and He knew that it would be in his tomb for at least three days before He would go into heaven to be with his Father. So by learning that, you knew that Jesus certainly wasn't telling the thief that he'd be with Him some place that He wasn't going to be? Jesus, Himself, didn't know when the Kingdom was to be established. When asked, He said that only His Father knew. Another reason He wouldn't have told the thief he'd be there that day. We need to be very careful to make certain that we don't just grab one verse of Scripture and rely on it without checking it against others.

"This thief had shown complete faith in Jesus and an understanding of who He was; he realized that Jesus was God's Son and that Jesus was assuring him...right that day

…that very minute… that he would be in the Kingdom. This thief could die knowing that he would be with Jesus when Jesus established Gods Kingdom, whenever that was to be. You and I know that the Kingdom hasn't even been established today… thousands of years later…and won't be till Jesus returns."

"Wow! You really have to know a lot about the Bible to find out all of that, don't you?"

"You never know it all. You never understand every word of the Bible. You can study it all of your life and always find something you'd failed to see before. The main thing to remember is that you need to study it constantly. There is really nothing more important in your life."

"Oh, Gammy, I want to. I just love my Bible…and thank you for the Concordance." She gave her grandmother another hug.

"Now, what is the Kingdom like, you ask? In the book of Revelation…the last book in the Bible…Jesus describes what this heavenly Kingdom on earth will be like and He informs John that it will last a thousand years."

"But I thought we were going to live forever. Is a thousand years forever?"

"It probably seems like it to you right now," she answered laughingly, "but the Kingdom goes on after the thousand years… it's just that Jesus will only be King for that long. After that…after all sin has been removed from the earth…He will turn the Kingdom over to His Father, God, and God will reign forever. You may want to look that up sometime in First Corinthians, chapter 15. In verse 24 it tells you that Jesus turns the Kingdom over to God, and in verse 28, it says that even Jesus will be under God's rule after that."

A puzzled look came over Breanna's face.

"But, Gammy, our pastor said that Jesus *is* God. That God turned Himself into a baby and came down to earth, but that Jesus is really God in the flesh." A frown came over her face.

"Breanna, I'm afraid we can't cover everything at one time. How about if we finish talking about what the Kingdom is like and then we can cover the subject of Jesus being God later?"

"But you're going home tomorrow and we won't have a chance." Tears started to wet her pretty eyes.

"Now, now," she consoled, "just because I'm going home, doesn't mean that we stop studying together. We can communicate by phone and e-mail and chat on line. I promise that as soon as I get home I'll write about God's relationship with Jesus, and we can study together that way. We can have our Bibles handy and you can ask all the questions you want. We won't stop discussing the Bible just because I'm in one place and you're in another. That will be the thing that will keep us close to each other. OK?"

"O.K." She wiped her eyes and settled back to try to understand what the kingdom would be like.

"Won't it be wonderful, Breanna...to see Jesus?"

"Gee, I can't imagine how great that would be. I bet He'll be a kind King."

"I'm sure He will be kind to those who believe in Him, but He will be firm with nonbelievers. There will be His saints...those who are 'in Him'...and there will be those on earth, still, who have not accepted Him."

"When do we get to be saints? Doesn't the Pope have to

make people saints?"

"That's what the Pope tells people, but that is not what the Bible tells us. When we believe who Jesus is, what He did for us and then we are baptized into Him, we become His saints. We do not need any pope to declare us such. In fact, God does not approve of a pope or even human priests."

"You're kidding?" She was astounded by her grandmother's declaration."You mean that God doesn't want the Catholics to have a pope and priests?"

"Honey, Catholic is a word that means universal and in the beginning of the church that is what the church was called. The Catholic Church was the Christian Church. But remember that John 4:24 tells us that we have to worship in Truth, and in Acts 2:42 that if we do not believe in the Jesus that the Apostles taught, we believe a lie. The Catholic church of today has strayed so far from the Truth about the Jesus that the Apostles taught, that it fits the description of the apostate church of prophesy."

"What is apostate, Gammy?"

"It means false…a false church."

"WOW! Where does the Bible describe the apostate church?"

"Well, there are several places that the Bible tells us what Believers should and shouldn't do, but let's finish with the Kingdom right now. I'd like to save the description of the Catholic Church and what it's beliefs are, until we get to the study of who Jesus really is. Is that OK with you?"

"I guess so."

Breanna was clearly disappointed not to be able to grasp everything at once, but the Catholic Church and its teachings were very important in the development of so many of the false doctrines that condemn Christendom, that her grandmother wanted to be sure that Breanna had plenty of time to absorb and understand it all.

"Honey, go to sleep tonight thinking of something positive. Close your eyes," she said, "remembering that by the time God comes to reign, all sin will have been removed from the earth. There will be no more crime; no more harshness; no more crippling diseases or illness; no more rage or unhappiness; no more terrorism. Just love and worship and music. I think that one of the most beautiful verses of the Bible is 1 Corinthians 2 verse 9. It tells us that no matter how beautiful we imagine it, or how wonderful we think it will be, we can't begin to know what God's Kingdom will be like." She opened her Bible to the passage and began to read.

*"It is written, the eye has not seen and the ear has not heard and the heart of man has not conceived the things which God has prepared for those who love Him."* She closed the book and smiled at Breanna.

The child was openly delighted at the prospect of such a Kingdom and was eager to look up, for herself, the Bible passages her grandmother recommended; verses that would tell her even more about God's Kingdom.

* * *

Before anyone else had awakened, Breanna was up and dressed. With her Bible and the list of verses her grandmother had given her. She had tiptoed down the stairs to the kitchen where she was now earnestly reading them for herself.

\* \* \*

"I don't want you to leave, Gammy," Breanna wept. "Can't you stay?"

"Now, Honey, you know I can't stay. I have my own home to look after and my church work to do. But remember, we're going to be e-mail pals....and you call me any time you feel like talking. How about a smile for me to take with me."

Breanna wiped her eyes and smiled at her grandmother, as her mom and dad stood patiently by. The attendant had already called for the passengers to board.

"Breanna, Gammy's got to get aboard now. Come over by the window where you can wave to her when she gets to her seat."

Gammy gave her son a hug, kissed her daughter-in-law, and leaned over to give Breanna a big squeeze. They backed away so Gammy could pass through the line, and moved to the window to see if they could see her once she was aboard. They couldn't, but they waved anyway. As the plane rolled away, they left the airport and Breanna cried softly all the way home.

# Chapter 7
# Who Is Jesus?

The flight home had been a good one. Conversation with the young soldier in the next seat had been pleasant and the food was certainly not the "horrible airline food" that had been described to her for years.

She had just risen from a good night's sleep, bathed and dressed, and was ready to get busy on the e-mail she had promised to send Breanna. Is Jesus God? Maybe she should give Breanna a little homework first. She wrote:

Dear Breanna,

I sure do miss you. I haven't forgotten my promise, but to help us get started on learning who Jesus is, maybe it would help if you made a list of all the places in the Bible that you can find the phrases:

God the Son

Incarnation (or God incarnate)

Or any verse that says that Jesus is God.

Also, tell me everything you know about God, and everything you know about Jesus. With those things, I will have a place to start. Don't be afraid to ask your pastor or

your Sunday school teacher to help you if you like. Kiss Mommy and Daddy for me, and know that I love you.
Gammy

She clicked on "send", knowing that Breanna would be pleased to hear from her so soon. She had a feeling that it wouldn't be long till Breanna sent back at least a part of the assignment. Learning who Jesus is would be the most important thing that the child would ever learn.

The balance of the day was spent in grocery shopping for some of the perishables she needed after being away; wiping away the dust that had made itself at home in her absence; and trying to catch up on some of the local news so that she could throw out the accumulation of newspapers that her neighbor had collected from her doorstep while she was away.

As usual, before she went to bed she checked her e-mail, and hearing the "You've got mail", knew there would be a message from Breanna. She wasn't disappointed.

Dear Gammy,

I found out what God is like. He's omnipotent, omniscient and omnipresent, and Gammy, I know what they mean. Omnipotent means Almighty...that God has all the power; Omniscient means He knows everything; and Omnipresent means that God is everywhere all the time. I asked my Sunday School teacher who God was, and that's what she told me. Is that right? God is also love. I'll do the other things, too, and send them to you as soon as I get them. I love you, Gammy.
Breanna

Her grandmother printed the e-mail and slipped it in the front of her Bible so that tomorrow, she could start working on teaching Breanna who Jesus is.

# Chapter 8
# My Father and I Are One

Her morning check of the e-mail brought another message from Breanna.

Dear Gammy,
When I went to Bible study last night, the preacher said that the Bible says that Jesus and God are one, so that means that Jesus is God. I looked in my Bible where he said it was (John chapter 10 verse 30), and I found it. Bye. I love you. Breanna.

Well, she thought, that's as good a place to start as any, so she took her Bible and the copies of Breanna's messages and settled down at her desk. This might take most of the day and would be too much to compose on the Internet, so she decided to do it on her word processor and cut and paste when it was ready to send.

Dearest Breanna,
I am going to start with the scripture you sent...John 10:30...where Jesus says that He and His Father are One. If

you had been told that Jesus was God… and you went searching for a scripture to prove that belief, wouldn't it be exciting to find this one? 'My Father and I are One.'

However, that is only one translation. If you go to, say, the Lamsa translation (from Aramaic, the language Jesus spoke) it says, 'my Father and I are of one accord.' This is a perfect example to use to explain to you that you cannot read one verse and decide the that one verse says it all. The Bible tells us, in 2nd Peter, Chapter 1, verse 20, that we must consider all the Scriptures together. We need to consider the circumstances at the time things are said; verses before and after the one we are reading; verses recorded at the same time or are written about the same event; who spoke the words; and to whom they were spoken.

Jesus is about to be crucified. In the previous verse, He is telling all who will listen who He is; why He came; and what it will take for us to be in His kingdom. He explains that He does everything that His Father wants Him to do…everything God commands Him to do…even to laying down His life. Then, in your King James version, He says, 'I and My Father are One'. In my Aramaic Version, He says, 'I and My Father are of one accord.' This is not *exactly* the same thing, is it? So you need to search a little further to determine whether Jesus and God are the same person….or whether Jesus and God are of the same accord…have the same purpose.

If you go to chapter 17 of John, verse 11, Jesus asks God to them keep those that are in Him….those that believe in Him and have been baptized…so that they might be 'one *as We are One*'. How can those who are followers of Jesus be one? Is Jesus asking God to make them God?..or to make them Jesus? Of course not. He is asking God to keep them in a way that will keep them obedient to His commandments (as He was obedient to His Father),so that they will be one with Him in the same way that He is one with His Father...that they will be of one accord...that they will have the same purpose...that they will be like Him.

"God instructs a couple getting married that they should be one. Does that mean that the husband becomes the wife?...or that the wife becomes the husband? God wants a man and his wife to be one in spirit, in purpose...to be in accord, one with the other.

Jesus told us that He was the Son of God. God told us that Jesus was His only begotten Son. What better proof do we need than that, to show that Jesus is the Son of God... not God in the form of His own Son. Don't forget what I told you about not having any contradictions in the Bible. There are lots of Scriptures that prove that Jesus couldn't have meant that He and His Father were actually God.

Remember you said that God was omnipotent...all powerful? And He is. But Jesus said, Himself, that He couldn't do anything without God's help. Does that sound like Jesus was all powerful?

Then your teacher told you that God was omnipresent...everywhere at once...and He is. But Jesus was not present except as any mortal man would be. He had to move from place to place just as His parents did...just as His disciples did. He was in one place at a time like any man would be.

You said God was omniscient...knew everything...and He is. But Jesus, Himself, said that there were things He,

Jesus, did not know…things that only God, His Father knew. He makes that clear in Mark 13, verse 32. Jesus was definitely not omniscient and never claimed to be. John Chapter 1, verse 18, explains that no one has seen God, but that Jesus came to declare God…and declare means to explain or to give evidence as a means of revealing God…to make a complete statement of or about His Father.

Knowing that there are no contradictions, think about these things and the 30th verse of John 10 and see if you now know what was being said? If you have any questions, call me.

Love, Gammy.

She highlighted the letter, clicked on "cut", went onto the Internet and pasted it into the e-mail form, punching "send". Before she could shut down her computer, the phone rang.

# Chapter 9
# God the Son or Son of God

Before she picked up the receiver she knew that it would be Breanna.

"Hello."

"Gammy! I have a question."

"Shoot."

"I used my Concordance to see if I could find some verses that said Jesus was God. God is listed so many times I don't know where to look. Can you tell me some of them?"

"Well, I just sent you an e-mail that might help you with some of them but let's see what I have at my finger tips. You know John 3, verse 16, where we are told that God so loved the world that He gave His only begotten Son that whoever believes in Him shall have everlasting life. That says that Jesus is God's Son."

"Oh, yeah, I remember that one."

"Do you remember what I told you begotten means?"

"To produce offspring."

"Yes, and John confirms it when he says, *'God's seed is in Him'*, talking about Jesus... *'He has been born of God'*. 1st Corinthians 3 verse 23 tells us that Christ is *God's*...not that

Christ is *God*. Another verse which I know you've heard many times is the one where God says, *'This is my beloved Son in whom I am well pleased'*. Again, God telling us that Jesus is His Son."

"Yep, I know that one."

"Do you believe that Jesus was a man, as God told us He was?"

"Yes."

"Do you believe, as all four Gospels tell us, that He was born of a woman?"

"Gospels"?

"Matthew, Mark, Luke and John."

"Of course…The Virgin Mary."

"Do you believe that He had a sinful nature just as we have?"

"He did?!"

"That's what the Bible tells us in Romans 8 verse 3. It tells us that God sent His Son in the likeness of sinful flesh."

"Then I believe it."

"Do you believe that he was tempted, just like we are?"

"Sure, I remember the Bible telling us that."

She seemed pleased that she had remembered reading that. She didn't remember that it was in Hebrews 4 verse 15, but that was not the important thing.

"And do you believe that Jesus was corruptible?"

"What does corruptible mean?"

"It means perishable…able to perish…that He was mortal…that He could die."

"Of course! He died for us"! Of this, she was sure.

"Well, if you believe that Jesus was a corruptible man, like the Bible tells us, and that He could be tempted as it also tells us, then He couldn't be God. James 1 verse 13 tells us that God cannot be tempted. Breanna, there are so many questions that you can ask…and look up the answers to… that can prove to you that Jesus was not God. I'll e-mail you a list tonight."

"OK. I'd like to have that."

"The Apostles knew that Jesus was the Son of God. Both God and Jesus had assured them of that. There was no thought in their minds that Jesus was God. That idea came about more than three hundred years after Jesus died. Paul tells us in 2 Corinthians 11, verses 4 and 13, that people will come who teach another Jesus whom the Apostles had not preached and a different gospel than what they had accepted. And he tells us that such teachings are false. Sweetheart, Truth doesn't change with time. Once God established the Truth, it remains firm and immovable. However, sometimes humans…and we know humans have sinful natures…often try to change the Truth into something that is more appealing to them; something that people want to hear or that best suits their own circumstances. That is what happened when humans decided that Jesus should be God the Son instead of the Son of God …as both Jesus and God told us He is.

"You can look up every single verse in your concordance with the word God and you will never find the phrase God the Son. God is not the Son, and the Son is *not* God. I think the Scriptures I e-mail you will show you that."

"Is saying Jesus is God what they mean by the Trinity?"

"Yes. That idea never entered the heads of the Apostles who knew and lived with Jesus, Himself. They knew that God had said, *'Before Me there was no God created, neither shall there be after Me. I, even I, am the Lord; and besides Me there is no Lord.'* To believe that Jesus is God is to drag God down, turn Him into the corruptible man that Jesus was, and worship Him as God.

"John 10 verse 33 tells us in clear, easy to understand words that Jesus was 'only a man', so Jesus couldn't be God. Then Numbers 23 verse 19 tells us in the same clear, easy to understand words that God was not a man, so He couldn't be Jesus. I'm afraid I gave you a project you can't achieve when I told you to find all the places that the Bible says, 'God the Son'. You won't find it. It isn't there."

"But Gammy, if Jesus isn't God, then why does almost everybody think He is?"

"Because the preachers and priests and pastors and evangelists have been drumming it into their heads from the time they were little children. The doctrine of the Trinity is the greatest brainwashing job in the history of mankind. Instead of going to the Scriptures and searching to see if what they are being taught is true, well intended people accept it to such a degree that, after awhile, they can't see the truth when they look at it. God gives them over to their sinful natures. This is what God calls *'hardening their hearts.'*"

"But why do the preachers and priests tell them these things if its not in the Bible?"

"Oh, they will tell you it's in the Bible. It's just that the verses they use to try to prove it, are what are called inferential verses. They develop the idea first, then they go searching for verses that can be inferred to support what they've developed."

79

"Like the one about 'My Father and I are One?'"

"Exactly. They quote only that one verse to their congregations to prove that Jesus is God. Those who hear it don't check it out to see that the following verses tell a different story. That's what happened in the development of the Doctrine of the Trinity."

"But how did it start, Gammy?"

It really seemed to bother the child, and her grandmother knew that this subject would be a full lesson in itself.

"Breanna, the development of the doctrine of The Trinity took a lot of years and, while it's an interesting process, it takes more study than we can do by phone or e-mail. How would you like to come visit me when school is out…"

"Oh, yes!" she interrupted.

"…then we can go out to lunch and then to the library where we'll have all the books we need to look up all you need to know about it. Would you like that?"

"Oh, Gammy, I'd love it!"

Her grandmother wasn't sure whether she was most excited about the studies that fascinated her, or the fact that her grandmother was going to take her out to lunch. Gammy was the only one who ever took her out to lunch.

"Gammy, Allison said I should be confessing my sins to a priest, or I will go to Hell."

"Allison?"

"Allison is my best friend."

"And she's a Roman Catholic?"

"Yes and she has to go to confession so she can go to heaven. She doesn't believe God's Kingdom is going to be on earth. Gammy, what is sinning?"

"Anytime we do things God wouldn't want us to do; say things God wouldn't want us to say; think things God wouldn't want us to think; we have sinned. All these things need to be confessed, but not to a man. God has appointed His Son as our High Priest and has told us that going to God, through Jesus, is the only way to forgiveness and salvation."

"The Bible says that Jesus is a priest?"

"It does. And it also says, in Revelation 1 verse 6, that when Jesus comes and sets up His kingdom, His saints...those of us who are saved... will be priests, too."

"Oh, yeah, I remember."

"When you are truly sorry for doing something that God wouldn't like...and you will try not to do it again...and if you go to God in the name of His Son, Jesus, and ask for forgiveness, you are forgiven. You don't have to ask over and over. You don't have to pay anything. You don't have to light any candles. You can know that you are forgiven, and God wants you to go about doing good, and not sinning the same sin again. He wants us to live our lives as nearly as we can, the way Jesus lived His....and the only way we can know how that is, is if we study the Bible and see what it tells us about Jesus' life."

"The Bible says all of that?"

"You bet it does. It says that Jesus became our high priest after he died sinless, and that it was to Him, not some earthly priest, we needed to go for forgiveness... that he is our go-between to God. Before we burn up the phone lines, let me speak to your mom."

Her scream, "MOM," nearly broke her grandmother's ear drum, but soon Michelle was on the phone. After they had exchanged the routine "How's everythings," Gammy spoke.

"Michelle, I didn't find the Truth until I was well into my seventies and it was difficult by then. Breanna is young and impressionable and I would really like to see her have an opportunity to base her belief on what is said in the Bible…not on what someone tells her is there."

"Well, I really just wanted her to have some religious training, and her little friend Allison is a Catholic, so that seemed a good place to send her."

"I think you should be careful what church you send her to. A false training can lead to a false belief, and that may be worse than no belief at all. Catholics discourage their members from reading the Bible, and for a very good reason. If they read the Bible, they will find that the Church is teaching false doctrines. Will you give me a few more months with her before you send her off to a Catholic school? She's doing so well in the Bible."

"Of course, Mom. She is so excited about what she's learning with you. I just thought that going to a church…any church…would enhance her understanding."

"I really think that if she studies more on her own, when she gets to the point where she can discern for herself what is Truth and what is fiction, she can make the choice as to which denomination she wishes to become a part. I hope you will discourage her from going to any church right now…at least till after she's spent the summer with me, will you?"

"Sure. Do you want to tell her? She's been sort of looking forward to going with Allison."

"Yes, I'll talk to her. Let me speak to her again."

"Hello, Gammy."

"Hi, Sweetheart. I've got a favor to ask."

"What?"

"Your mom tells me that you're planning to go to church with Allison."

"Uh Huh."

"Will you not do that until after you spend time with me this summer?"

"Why?"

"Well, do you remember all the things that we've been talking about….how some churches teach things that aren't in the Bible?"

"Uh huh, I remember."

"Well, I'd like for you not to start hearing these things until you have already studied your Bible to the point that you'll be able to know, when they tell you something, whether or not its true. I think that between now and the time you've spent the summer with me…"

"Oh," she almost screamed, "can I spend the *whole* summer with you?"

"I look forward to it. And by the end of the summer, I think you'll be at a point where you can decide what church you want to join…I think you'll know what you believe. What do you say?"

"OK. Allison says some crazy things anyway."

"Well, after we've studied awhile, maybe you'll be able to help Allison understand her Bible better."

"She doesn't have a Bible, Gammy."

"Well, maybe we can get her one."

"Oh, yes, let's. Then we'll be able to study together."

"That will be something to look forward to. Breanna, I'm

going to send you those Scriptures I mentioned, but you'd better hang up now, before your folks go broke." They both laughed, said their goodbyes and placed the receivers in their cradles.

* * *

Her grandmother went to her computer, opened Microsoft Word and began to type.

Breanna, dearest.

Here are a few of the Scriptures that you might want to study in making your determination as to whether Jesus is God....or is God's Son.

Hebrews 2 verse 9. If Jesus is God, how could He be lower than the angels? Could God be lower than the angels?

Philippians 2 verse 8. If Jesus is God, to whom did He have to become obedient?

Hebrews 5 verse 8. If Jesus is God, what did He have to learn? God would already know everything, wouldn't He?

Hebrews 1 verse 4. If Jesus is God, why would He have to be made better than the angels. Wouldn't God already be better than the angels?

Luke 2 verse 52. If Jesus is God, why would it be necessary for Him to'increase' in wisdom and stature and in favor with God?

Hebrews 5 verse 9. If Jesus is God, why would He have to be 'made' perfect? Isn't God already perfect?

John 5 verse 30. If Jesus is God, why couldn't He do anything on His own?

Psalm 5 verse 4. If Jesus is God, then the Bible lies when

it says that God cannot dwell in the presence of sin. Jesus was born into this sinful world, with a sinful nature, to make it possible for us to have salvation.

John 14 verse 28. If Jesus is God, why would He tell us that God was greater than He. Wouldn't they be the same?

Revelation 22 verse 16. If Jesus is God, how could He be the offspring of David? Could immortal God be the offspring of a mortal man?

Hebrews 2 verse 11. If Jesus is God, does that mean that when we are baptized, we will be brethren of God?

1st John 3 verse 9. If Jesus is God, why are we told that He is "born *of* God", not that He is "born *as* God"?

1st Corinthians 3 verse 23. If Jesus is God, how can He belong to God?

John 5 verse 30. If Jesus is God, wouldn't they both have the same will? How can there be two separate wills in one God?

John 1 verse 18. If Jesus is God, isn't it calling the Bible a liar when it says that *"no man hath seen God at any time"*…after we are told that Jesus *"dwelt among us"*?

John 5 verse 27. If Jesus is God, why did He have to be given authority by God? Wouldn't He, as God, already have had authority?

Philippians 2 verse 9. If Jesus is God, why did He need to be highly exalted and who exalted Him?

Mark 13 verse 32. If Jesus is God, wouldn't He know everything that God knows, and why would He say that he doesn't know when the end will come…only the Father knows?

1st Corinthians 15 verses 24 and 28. If Jesus is God, how

could He become a subject under God, just as all of us will be when the thousand year kingdom is complete?

Isaiah 42 verse 1 and chapter 49 verse 5. In these Old Testament Scriptures, God tells us that He is sending Jesus to be His servant; and then in

Matthew, 12 verse 18. The confirmation that Jesus is God's servant. Does that sound like they are equal?

Honey, study all these verses and try to understand what they are telling you.

I love you.

Gammy

She highlighted the document, clicked on the "cut" icon; went on line; pasted the message; and hit the send button. It had been a long day and she was ready for bed.

# Chapter 10
## School Tragedy

She couldn't believe that she had slept till nine o'clock. She must have been more weary than she thought. As she put her feet into her slippers and headed for the bathroom, she flipped on the television to catch the top-of-the-hour news. When she reached the door, something stopped her in her tracks. The words "Adamstonville Elementary School" caught her attention. That was where Breanna attended school.

She wheeled around, sat on the edge of the bed and watched with horror as pictures were shown of children running in all directions while the sound of gunshots could be heard. Her heart was in her throat as she reached for the phone.

The news commentator began again.

"The pictures you are seeing were filmed about an hour ago, when a boy, just as students were entering the building, began to shoot at his classmates, wounding several and killing at least one. The boy's identity is not being revealed at this time."

She could tell that Greg's phone was ringing, but there was no answer. She was glued to the television, trying Greg's number every few minutes…or was it every few seconds? Finally, Michelle answered. It was obvious from her voice, that she was upset and out of breath.

"Michelle, is Breanna alright?"

"You saw the TV? Physically, she is all right. I don't know how this will affect her emotionally. The child that was killed was Breanna's friend, Cathy Abbelle, and she was holding Breanna's hand when she was hit. When I arrived at the school later to pick Breanna up, she was still trembling and the nurse had given her a sedative to try to calm her down. She can't seem to stop crying."

"Where is she now?"

"She's right here…we just walked into the house when the phone rang. Would you like to talk to her?"

"Please."

Breanna came to the phone. She was apparently upset, but her weeping had subsided. When she realized who was on the line, she spoke. "Oh, Gammy. It was awful. We weren't doing anything….he just started shooting, and Cathy fell down…. I didn't even see the blood." She drew in a deep breath and continued. "She just laid there like she was asleep. Then the teacher came running over and grabbed her up and told me to follow her. That was when I saw the blood dripping on the walkway. I was so scared, Gammy", and she began to sob.

"I know you were scared, Honey. I'd have been scared, too. But I'm so glad that you weren't hurt. When I heard the newscast, I was so afraid for you. Are you all right, Honey?"

"Yes, Gammy," she whimpered through her sniffles, "I'm OK."

"Does anyone know why the boy decided to do such a thing? Had he said anything?"

"He said the Devil made him do it. Can the Devil make people do things like that?"

"We'll talk about that, but right now I think your mom wants you to take a warm bath and try to get some rest. Will you do that for me?"

"OK. Bye, Gammy," and Michelle came on the line.

"They are having counselors at school in the morning to help the children through this. I think I need counseling as much as Breanna does. When I heard this on TV, I nearly died before I could get there to find out that she was all right."

"I had the same reaction. Oh, Michelle, how can children kill one another? What has this world come to? Aren't they taught *anything* about right and wrong?"

"I know, Mom, you have to wonder what our children are developing into."

"Well, you go help Breanna get settled. I just wanted to be sure she was all right. She seems to think that the young man was prompted by the Devil. I have a lot to say to her about that, so I'd better get to work on it. Do take care of yourself. I assume you've called Greg?"

"Oh, yes. The minute I got to the school and found out that she was all right, I gave him a call. He hadn't heard about the shooting, thank goodness."

"Yes, that was a blessing. I'll talk to you tomorrow. Bye, dear."

"Bye, Mom."

First things first. Gammy dropped to her knees beside her bed and thanked God for protecting Breanna in this incident.

She also prayed for the shooter…and for his parents. She knew that they must be suffering terribly…that their hearts must be breaking. And she prayed for those left by the child that was killed.

# Chapter 11
# The Devil

The Devil? How could she explain that well known creature....who wasn't really known at all...to Breanna. It was important! Perhaps she should write her a letter so that she could read it when she had time...and keep it to read again and again as others would doubtless challenge her about "his" existence. Here goes!

Dearest Breanna,

Poor ole Devil. Everyone wants to blame him for everything that goes wrong in the world, and guess what. The Devil is to blame. The problem is that most people don't realize what the devil is.

Think back, Breanna, to what the Bible tells us about the world when it was first created. In Genesis 1 verse 31, it tells us that *"God saw everything that he had made, and behold, it was very good."* Even the serpent, whom many call the Devil, was good because it had not yet sinned. Where was the devil, as we know it? It didn't exist.

Then, even when sin had entered the world, there was no mention of a devil, but man did not remain in his very good state, but developed evil inclinations. We're told that in Genesis 6 verse 5. What caused the change? Not a supernatural devil, but *Sin.*

The devil isn't the supernatural, spiritual being that dwells inside of us, making us do sinful things as most people think. Devil is a word…not a person. This personification of sin is blamed for all the evil in the world. Do you know what personification means? It means that you refer to something that is *not* a person, as though it *were* a person.

But God tells us that there is no outside force that makes us do evil. It all comes from inside of us. The Bible says, *"What comes out of a man, that defiles a man. For from within, out of the heart of men, proceed evil thoughts, adultries, fornications, murders, thefts, covetousness, wickedness, deceit, lewdness, and evil eye, blasphemy, pride, foolishness. All these evil things come from within and defiles a man."* That's in Mark 7, verses 18 through 23 in case you want to look it up.

In verse 18 He had said that, *"There is nothing outside of a man…that can defile him."* That means that there is no Devil-person that causes people to do the evil things that they do.

What we are being told is that man has a sinful nature. Even Jesus was born with a sinful nature. When the Bible speaks of man, it is speaking of human beings. Mortals. There is no one but ourselves that we can blame for the evil we do. *"…each one is tempted when he is drawn away by his own desires…"*, not by a person called the Devil. Psalms 10 verse 2 tells us in simple words that *"the wicked is snared in the work of his own hands."* Again, we have no one to blame

GRANDMA, DO PREACHERS LIE?

but ourselves for the evil *WE* do.

When we know…because God tells us…that *"every thought in man's heart is evil, continually"*, we should be able to understand that all the evil things we do, *WE* do!

If we go to the New Testament, we know that Paul explained that though he knew what was right, and wanted to do the right thing, he often did things that he didn't want to do. He knew that he was of the flesh…that he had a sinful nature…and he told the Believers in the church at Rome that, *"it is not I who do it, but sin which dominates me."*. That's sin…not a devil person.

Devil, serpent and Satan are all names man has given the evil one.

The serpent was the creature in the Garden of Eden that convinced Eve to disbelieve God's warning that death would follow if they ate of the tree of Knowledge of Good and Evil. It was an upright, speaking and thinking creature (probably the most intelligent creature after man) but because it sinned by deceiving Eve into believing that God did not mean what He said, God destined it (and all its descendants) to crawl on it's belly and eat dust. If it's crawling on it's belly, it doesn't fit the description people give to the Devil-person they believe exists. True, it (not he but it ) introduced sin into the world through Adam and Eve, but God tells us that that creature, and all of its descendants, will always be crawling around in the dust. I think we can dismiss the serpent as some supernatural, spiritual person, causing us to sin.

Man has never wanted to accept responsibility for his own sinfulness, and making sin into a supernatural being and naming it, relieves man of his own responsibility and gives him something ...someone...on whom to blame his own natural evil conduct. Remember, Devil is a word, not a person.

Then there's Satan. Another person of man's imagination. Satan like Devil is a word, not a person. It is a Greek word and means adversary; or one who is against or opposes something or someone.

When Jesus was about to be crucified, Peter tried to talk Him into saving Himself, but Jesus knew what God wanted His fate to be. He said to Peter, *"Get thee behind me Satan..."* (Look that up in Matthew 16, verse 23). Jesus wasn't calling Peter, this man He had chosen to be one of His Apostles and a leader in establishing His church, an evil, super natural instigator of evil in the world. He goes on, in the next few words of that verse to tell Peter that he was an offense to Him. Peter was an offense in that he was opposing God's will that Jesus must die.

Adam, the very first man, blamed God for giving him Eve and then blamed Eve for giving him the fruit of the Tree of Knowledge of Good and Evil, saying, *"The woman whom You gave to be with me, she gave me of the tree..."*(Genesis. 3 verse 12)

It has been that way ever since. Man must blame someone else for his sinful nature, so the Devil was created as a scapegoat...not by God, but by man.

Any Christian who says that there is a devil-being (in whatever form) that has supernatural power over man is saying that this being is more powerful than God, whose spirit we profess to have in us. I don't think I want to be one of the people who says such a thing, and I don't think you do either.

Yes, Breanna, there is a Devil…and we need only to look in a mirror to see it.

Your schoolmate who shot Cathy and his other classmates was doing it of his own free will. He may have tried to blame someone else…some person may have influenced him…some person may have even made the suggestion…but when it came down to pulling the trigger, he did that of his own free will. There is no supernatural, evil one that makes a person do such things.

Honey, we need to pray, not only for Cathy's folks and for those that are injured, but we need to pray for the boy who did this awful thing. We need to pray for his family, too. Don't you know how sad they must be?

If there is anything you can't understand about this, please feel free to give me a call (or use our faithful e-mail). I so much want you to understand this completely.

Much love, Sweetheart.

Gammy

# Chapter 12
## Face to Face With Death

All of the TV channels were filled with the story of the school shooting. The young boy…only nine…was identified in spite of his age, and pictures of him were shown on the screens. He was such a child. They also showed a picture of Cathy, the only victim who lost her life. Gammy remembered having seen her with Breanna when she was visiting them the week before. What a tragedy. Her heart ached for all of them.

She dialed Breanna's number and her dad answered the phone.

"Hi, Greg, how is Breanna?"

"She's handling it better than her mother…and certainly better than I am. I'm glad I didn't know about it till it was over. I've been just sick as it is."

"Is she nearby? Could I speak to her?"

"Sure". And he turned and called to Breanna, who couldn't have been far away. She was on the phone in seconds.

"Hi, Gammy."

"Hi, Sweetie, I'm so glad you're holding up OK. Have you seen Cathy's folks?"

"I haven't, but Mom and Dad went over just before dinner and took them a casserole. Mom said that they were really upset and crying."

"Of course they are. Can you imagine how your mom and dad would feel if they lost you? Do they have any other children?"

"No, Cathy was their only child."

"In a few months, when the initial shock has passed, maybe you can drop by and see them from time to time. Maybe you can sort of fill some of the place in their hearts left by Cathy's death."

"I'll try, Gammy. I have a lot of pictures of Cathy and me. She was one of my best friends." Breanna began to cry softly.

"Breanna, don't ever forget the good times the two of you had…and much later, maybe you can share some of those pictures and stories with her parents."

"I won't forget, Gammy, and I will."

"I mailed you a letter today explaining about the Devil. I want you to study it…and to study your Bible where it talks about it. You should learn exactly what your Bible says about the Devil."

"OK."

"And, Honey, be sure to let me know if there is any part of it you don't understand. Will you do that?"

"Yes, Gammy, I will."

"I love you, Honey, now let me speak to your mom."

When Michelle came to the phone and greeted her mother-in-law, she asked if Breanna was really doing OK.

"I think so, Mom. I guess she is young enough that the fact of death is not so real as it is to those of us who are adults. She talks a lot about Cathy, but the fact that she was actually holding her hand when she was killed doesn't seem to have made any devastating impact on her...at least, not yet. The newspaper and television people keep trying to interview her, but I won't let them near her."

"Good! I think you're wise about that. I was surprised not to have seen her, though several commentators have reported that a friend had been holding the girl's hand at the time she was shot. One even gave Breanna's name, but I was glad not to have seen her dragged out in front of the world to be reminded of the horror."

"Greg and I agree that we're not going to allow it."

"Well, Honey, I just wanted to check on you folks and make sure everything was all right. Call me if you need me, will you?"

"Of course, Mom. And thanks for your call."

# Chapter 13
## An Invitation to Grandmother's House

Gammy had not been able to tear herself away from the television. Now the cameras had been placed in front of Greg's house and she knew that they were not having a moments peace. It was Breanna they wanted to see…wanted to film…wanted to torment with questions. How could they be so thoughtless. Michelle had said that they were there from early morning till dark. The child had to do her school work at home to avoid leaving the house and facing this barrage.

She reached for the phone and dialed Greg's number. Michelle answered the phone.

"Hi, Michelle, I see your house is in the news."

"Oh, Mom, it's so awful. They are determined to catch Breanna."

"I had a thought that you might want to consider. There's a flight from Adamstonville at about midnight that gets here at 5:30 in the morning. Why don't you get Breanna's assignments from school, pack her books and some clothes and send her to me till this all settles down? It will give you and Greg more freedom, too."

"Gee, Mom. Are you sure you want to do that? I know

Breanna would love it and Greg and I could sure use the relief. We haven't even been able to go to work."

"I'd love having her, Michelle, and I know she'd enjoy being here. Just let me know when she will arrive and I'll be at the airport to pick her up."

"Thanks, Mom. I'll talk to Greg, but I'm sure he'll like the idea. I'll e-mail you her time of arrival. The cameras are all gone by dark, so it shouldn't be a problem getting her to the airport. I suspect, knowing that she's going to your house, we won't have any trouble keeping her awake, either."

They both laughed and said their goodbyes.

# Chapter 14
# Preparing For Breanna's Visit

YOU'VE GOT MAIL!

Hi, Gammy.

I will be leaving tomorrow night to come be with you. I'm so excited. I just got your letter about the Devil, so I will bring it with me and we can talk about it then. OK? And can we go out to lunch and the library and talk about the Trinity?

I get there at 5:30 Friday morning, on A-1 Airline, so you'll have to get up early, won't you?

I love you.

P. S. I'll bring my Bible and Concordance, too.

Her grandmother spent most of the day cleaning the guest room, and changing the sheets, which weren't soiled but hadn't been changed nor slept on in months. She pulled out the pretty pink bedspread that Breanna liked so well and used pink sheets to match. Removing all the odds and ends that would mean nothing to Breanna, she replaced them with the few "girlie" things she had around the house, and put her old-fashioned doll on the bed. Breanna would like that.

Her next project was to go shopping for foods that would be appealing to the child. She, herself, ate very little and almost no sweets or fat. She was sure that none of the choices she made for herself would pique Breanna's appetite. In fact, she might have to fall off her own regime while Breanna was with her....just a little.

Once the house was ready and the refrigerator stocked, she did her evening Bible readings, said her prayers, and was ready for bed. It had been a good day.

# Chapter 15
# Homosexuality

It was still dark when she got out of bed at 4:30 a.m. The airport wasn't far away, but she wanted to give herself plenty of time to get there before Breanna's plane actually arrived. She was pleased that she would have this time with her granddaughter.

The first people to deplane were Breanna and the attendant that was holding her hand. They were giggling together, so it was obvious that it had been a good flight.

"Hi, Gammy. This is Shari. She gave me extra goodies and cokes." She was smiling ear to ear.

"Hello, Shari. Thank you for taking such good care of her. She's very special to me."

"I can understand that. She's a very special young lady. She even told me a bit about the Bible."

Breanna and Shari said their good byes and Gammy took Breanna's bag, leaving her to carry her own books. They settled into the little Honda and headed for Gammy's house... Breanna chattering all the way about all the newspeople who were hounding her folks.

"But", she said, "the police told me that I shouldn't talk to them about what happened, so I don't want to."

"Well, I'm so glad you get to be with me for awhile. I think we'll have a lot of fun and you won't have to worry about having to hide from the press."

"Yeah!" And she smiled up at her grandmother.

* * *

After Breanna was all settled in the room her grandmother had prepared for her (and which, incidentally, she "luv'd") her grandmother prepared breakfast and they sat down to devour the cinnamon rolls and hot chocolate. They decided they wouldn't do any studying today…they'd just relax.

It was during their midday snack that her grandmother noticed that Breanna looked pensive. She seemed to want to ask a question, but did not know how to begin. She hoped that she was not homesick.

"Breanna, is something bothering you?" She did not take her eyes off of the child, and Breanna looked at her grandmother but did not seem to know how to answer. Gammy just continued to look into her eyes affectionately, and finally the question popped out.

"Gammy, what is a 'fag'?"

It was all that she could do to keep from showing her shock at the question, but she knew that there must be some reason beyond curiosity that Breanna would ask the question and she wanted to answer her in a helpful way. "Honey, do you know what homosexual means?"

"Not really."

"It's a person who feels and, in most instances, exercises sexual desires for a person of the same sex. A man for a man or a woman for a woman."

"Is that being gay?"

"When a man shows a sexual interest in another man or a woman is drawn, sexually, to another woman, they are called homosexuals. Yes, they're called gay, and the slang, and more insulting language, for homosexuals is *fag*. Why do you ask?"

"That's what all the kids at school called Billy," she answered matter of factly.

"Did you?"

"Oh, no, Gammy. I could tell by the way they talked, and how unhappy it made Billy, that it wasn't a very nice thing to be saying. Gammy, is it a sin to call him a fag…or is it a sin to be a homo…?"

"A homosexual? Why don't we see what the Bible says about it?"

"Does the Bible say something about homosexuals?"

"The Bible says something about just about anything you can think of. Look up the word in your Concordance. I know we said we were going to wait till tomorrow to start our studies, but would you like to spend a little while on this subject now?"

"Let's do. I can't believe the Bible talks about that."

"Honey, the Bible teaches us about any subject that could make a difference in our lives. Run get your books."

Breanna went up the stairs two at a time and returned with both books in her arms. She bounced onto the sofa and opened her Concordance. "H-o-m-o…" she paused.

"s-e-x-u-a-l," Gammy prompted.

Breanna looked at the page, looked up at her grandmother,

and back to the book again.

"It isn't here! God didn't say anything about homosexuals!"

"He may not have used that particular word, but let's see if we can find it another way."

She reached into the bookcase at her right and pulled out a paperback book entitled, *Where to Find It in the Bible.*

"Sometimes," she continued as she began to turn the pages, "the words we use today are not the words used in biblical times."

When she reached the page containing the word, she handed Breanna a pen and and gave her a gentle instruction.

"At the top of the page of your Concordance, where the word homosexual would have alphabetically been, write homosexual, colon, see page 245 in *Where to Find It in the Bible.*"

"Gee, thanks, Gammy," she said as she made the notation.

"Here, here's a blank sheet of paper. Let's make a list of the places we're told we will find something on the subject. The first scripture listed is Genesis 19, verse 5." Taking her Bible and turning to the scripture, she read aloud. " '*And they called to Lot and said to him, Where are the men who came to you tonight? Bring them out to us that we may know them carnally'.* That means that they wanted to know them sexually…that is, to have sex with them. Do you know the story of Lot?"

"Isn't he the one who was saved from Sodom and his wife turned to a pillar of salt?"

"That's the one. God sent two men…two messengers…and what are God's messengers called?"

"Angels!"

"That's right. God sent them to Lot to warn him that He was going to destroy the city. The reason God was so unhappy with the city was because there was so much sin there and nearly all the men were homosexuals. When they saw these two strange men going into Lot's house, they immediately tried to get Lot to turn them over to them. Of course, Lot refused. He was the only person in that city whom God considered good enough to save."

"How about his wife?"

"Nothing in the Scriptures tells us that the attempt to save his wife was because she was good. In fact, she was probably saved because of Lot's righteousness. We know that his wife disobeyed God after He had told her not to look back."

"Gammy, that doesn't seem right to me. I can't see how anyone can be turned into salt."

Her grandmother laughed heartily. She had had the same problem with that verse for nearly seventy-five years…until she learned how to do Bible research.

"Breanna, do you know what Americans mean when they say someone *kicked the bucket?*"

"Sure, it means they died."

"If you were from another country and were learning to speak English, you'd learn what kick meant and you'd learn what a bucket was, but if someone said that another person had kicked the bucket , do you think they would have known that it meant they died?"

She thought for a moment. "I guess not."

"The phrase *kicked the bucket* is an idiom meaning that someone died. Well, in Aramaic, the phrase *turned to a pillar of salt* is an idiom that means that the person is petrified with fear and died."

"Wow! That makes more sense."

"Once we know that, we also learn two other things. One, we know why God told her not to look back. Imagine how you would feel if you looked back at the city where your children were and saw it burning…saw your own children being completely destroyed. It would be enough to create a petrifying fear…and certainly enough to cause death.

"Secondly, we know that her death was not God's punishment for disobeying, it was the consequences of that disobedience. God instructed her not to look back because He knew the affect it would have on her."

"Yeeeah! Now I understand. I wish the Bible would tell us some of these things."

"Well, if you check in more than one translation, sometimes they do. In fact, as a footnote to this scripture in the Lamsa translation, it does explain that."

She held her Bible out so that Breanna could read the footnote. The child smiled. It was as though a light had gone on in her head.

"Now, back to your study. The next scripture that's listed, Leviticus 18 verse 22, is a commandment from God to the men of the nation. He says, *'You shall not lie with a man as with a woman; because it is an abomination'*. In chapter 20, verse 13, God continues by saying, *'If a man lies with a male as he lies with a woman, both of them have committed an abomination; they shall surely be put to death.'* God uses the word abomination when he is most disgusted…when he truly hates something. Even though He does not use the word homosexuality, it is clear that God despises it."

"He really does hate it doesn't He?"

"There are a number of other verses that make it just as clear, and not just men. In Romans 1 verses 26 through 28, we're told that *'even the women exchanged what is the natural use for what is against nature.'* God created woman to be a helpmate of man and to bear children. That is the natural use that God refers to. To use their bodies as a way of satisfying sexual lusts with another woman, was against God's will and purpose for their lives. *'Likewise,'* He continues, *'also the men, leaving the natural use of the woman, burned in their lust for one another, men with men committing what is shameful..God gave them over to a debased mind, to do those things which are not fitting'.* Do you know what that is saying God is doing to these homosexuals?"

"I don't think so."

"What they are doing is so shameful…so horrible in God's eyes…that He is going to give up on them and let them continue in their sinful ways, and they will never see God's Kingdom."

"You mean they can't have salvation at all?" She seemed distressed at the thought.

"God makes that clear in First Corinthians 6, verses 9 -11, though there is always the chance that one might change his ways, and ask forgiveness. Unfortunately, seldom does a homosexual do so."

From her Bible she read to Breanna. *"…the unrighteous will not inherit the kingdom of God. Do not be deceived. Neither fornicators, nor idolaters, nor adulterers, nor men who lie with males...will inherit the kingdom of God'."*

"And men who lie with males are homosexuals, aren't they?"

"The Concordance usually has all words that appear in any translation of the Bible. I'm not sure how they missed homosexual, because here in the New King James Version, the word homosexuals is used in verse 9.

"Gee, it does say that, doesn't it?"

"OK, does that answer your question about the word fag?"

Breanna hung her head, but said nothing. Neither did her grandmother. Then, after a few minutes, the little girl looked up with tears in her eyes and Gammy took her in her arms and held her close while she wept.

When the tears were over, Breanna wanted to know if her grandmother thought that Billy had been shooting because people called him a fag.

"That could certainly have contributed to the unhappiness he must have been feeling to be able to do such a thing. It isn't an excuse, of course, but many things contribute to distress and despair, and people so young don't always have someone to help them deal with such problems. Are both of his parents at home?"

"I don't think he has a father...I mean, I don't think his father lives with them, and I know his mother works two jobs."

Her grandmother put her arms around the girl's shoulders, held her close for a moment, then asked if they'd had enough studying for the day and suggested they take a trip to the zoo...and an afternoon milkshake. The invitation was accepted without hesitation.

# Chapter 16
# The Trinity

After breakfast on Saturday, Gammy asked whether Breanna wanted go to lunch and work on the Trinity.

"Oh, let's!"

"I wonder why I knew you were going to say that," Gammy answered with a smile.

Breanna smiled, too.

Each of them straightened their own rooms and made their own beds; they brushed their teeth; selected their clothes for the day; showered (one at a time) and got themselves dressed. Breanna e-mailed her Mom that she had arrived o.k. (although her grandmother had already done so) and told her what their plans were for the day. The morning passed quickly and, not surprisingly, Breanna was ready for lunch even before the clock struck noon.

"Where would you like to go for lunch?"

"I want to go to Jack-in-the-Box!"

"Jack-in-the-Box? That's where you want to go?"

"Sure, Gammy, they have the best egg rolls in the whole world."

"Well, I'll just have to have some of those best-in-the-world egg rolls, I guess."

While she hadn't been there before, she knew where it was. It's hard to miss it if you drive through town. No, she didn't want anything else, just three egg rolls, so Gammy ordered the same for herself. They ordered diet cokes and Breanna informed the young lady at the counter that her grandmother wanted a senior coke. The girl smiled and deducted fifty cents off the price of one of the cokes.

Breanna was right. Her grandmother had had egg rolls in many different Chinese restaurants, but these were the best she had tasted.

"Thank you, Breanna, for introducing me to Mr. Box."

Breanna thought this was the funniest thing she'd ever heard and almost fell off her seat, repeating over and over, "Mr. Box! Mr. Box! Mr. Box!".

"OK, have you had enough to eat? Shall we have some ice cream later on, after we've had some time in the library?"

"Yeah, that's great." She was still laughing at Mr.Box as they cleared off their table and left the restaurant.

Cannonson was a small town, but because they had their Bibles and notebooks, they decided to drive rather than walk to the county library. They settled themselves, not feeling guilty or selfish for having taken one of the largest tables because there was almost no one else there.

"Breanna," her grandmother asked, "do you believe that Jesus was a human being, just as we are human beings?"

"Sure. That's what we found out in our Bibles, remember?"

Her grandmother had to smile. "Well, if you believe that Jesus was a corruptible man, like the Bible tells us, then all you need to do is read Romans 1, verses 23 and 32 to know that worshiping Jesus as God is the same as worshiping an idol."

Before she had completed the sentence, Breanna had turned to Romans 1 and was reading it for herself.

"Isn't that what it says, Breanna?"

" '*Professing to be wise, they became fools, and changed the incorruptible God into an image made like corruptible man.* '" She looked quizzically at her grandmother, then spoke.

"Who is the 'they' its talking about…the ones that thought they were wise but became fools?"

"Sweetheart, you remember that I told you that truth doesn't change with time. Once God established the Truth, it remains firm and immovable. However, sometimes humans…and we know humans have sinful natures…often try to change the Truth into something that is more appealing to them. Something that people want to hear or that best suits their own circumstances. That is what happened when humans…more specifically those in the church…decided that Jesus should be God the Son instead of the Son of God."

"The Trinity?"

"Yes. That idea never entered the heads of the Apostles because, you remember, they knew that God had said, '*Before Me there was no God created, neither shall there be after Me. I, even I, am the Lord; and besides Me there is no Lord.* ' To believe that Jesus is God is to drag God down, turn Him into the corruptible man that Jesus was, and worship Him as God. God calls this idol worship, and He hates it."

"You mean that people that believe that Jesus is God, won't be in God's Kingdom?" She seemed stunned.

"Well, if you read on you'll see that when you exchange the Truth of God for the lie, and worship and serve Jesus, who is the creature that God made, instead of worshiping God the creator, God gives them up to vile passions and all sorts of problems result. In the end, God said, *'They are deserving of death'."*

"They won't have everlasting life if they worship Jesus as God?"

"The Bible is God's instruction book to us, Breanna. We all have to search out, for ourselves, the Truth of what is there. To me it says that to worship Jesus as God is idol worship, and God abhors an idol worshiper. I can't imagine Him letting one into His eternal kingdom."

"Me either."

Her eyes fell to her Bible and she continued reading the balance of Romans 1. After a few moments, she cocked her head to one side, looked her grandmother in the eye, and asked an expected question. "Gammy, if Jesus isn't God, then why does almost everybody think He is?"

"Come with me."

They put their Bibles, worksheets and pencils down side by side, and together went to the reference shelves to select the books with which they would be working.

"OK, Breanna, from each set of encyclopedias, let's get the book that gives us the word Trinity. You get the *Britannica*…and you can see right on the edge which book has the letter 'T' I'll get the *Americana* and the *Colliers*."

They busied themselves collecting the three large books and put them on the table with their Bibles.

"I think we have all we can handle for awhile."

Breanna settled on the chair next to her grandmother.

"All right, here we go. Let's start with the *Encyclopedia Britannica*. That's the one like you have at home. What does that say about the Trinity?"

Breanna leafed through the book until she found Trinity. She laid the open book between them and began to read. "'Trinity, a Christian doctrine, the unity of Father, Son and Holy Spirit as three persons in one Godhead'." She looked at her grandmother. "Doesn't Godhead mean three?"

"No, Godhead means the quality or state of being divine...which God is. Applying it to the Trinity was a man-designed explanation of the word."

"Then I don't understand."

"I'm not surprised. Continue with what is said about it."

"'Neither the word Trinity nor the explicit doctrine appears in the New Testament, nor did Jesus and his followers intend to contradict the Shema in the Old Testament: *'Hear, O Israel: The Lord our God is one Lord'*. Doesn't that say that it's not in the Bible? That Jesus isn't a part of a Trinity?"

"It goes on to tell us," and her grandmother took the book, "that the doctrine developed over several centuries. It was something that the heads of the church fought over for many, many years." She looked at the book and began to read. "'It was not until the fourth century, that the distinctness of the three and their unity were brought together in a single orthodox doctrine of one essence and three persons'."

"I don't understand at all, Gammy."

"Me either. Let's see what the Americana has to say." She laid aside the open book from which she had been reading and opened the *Encyclopedia Americana* to Trinity.

"Here, Breanna. This one tells you why you don't understand. 'It is held that although the doctrine is beyond the grasp of human reason, it is, like many of the formulations of physical science, not contrary to reason, and may be apprehended (though it may not be comprehended) by the human mind'. Does that help you to understand?"

"I'm afraid not, Gammy."

"Of course it doesn't. And nothing that can be said will make it understandable, and God has something to say about that, too."

"About understanding?"

"Yes, about understanding. The Bible tells us over and over again, how important it is to understand the teachings of Jesus. We're told that it is like speaking into the air to speak things that are not understood. Before you ask, it's 1 Corinthians 14, verse 9." They both laughed.

"Breanna, churches that teach the Trinity are deceiving themselves and their congregations, and they will die for it. But not only them, but those who hear what they teach and do not search the Scriptures to see if what they teach is true."

"Do you know where it says that?"

"Sure, several places. In 2 Peter 2, verses 1 and 2 we're told of the destruction of those who teach falsely; Matthew 13, verse 19 tells us that if we can't understand what we are taught, it can't take root in our hearts and we will be denied access to the Kingdom; and in both Acts 17, verse 11 and John 5, verse 39 we are reminded of the duty to search out the Truth for ourselves.

"The Bible is full of verses that express the need for understanding, and if you look them up in your Concordance some time, I think you'll be surprised at just how many.

"If we can't understand the Trinity, Breanna, we can be sure that it isn't God's word. The Trinity is a doctrine developed by man, not by God, however, it might help to know how it got started.

"See right here," she said, pointing, "it tells us that the doctrine of God in the Old Testament was that God is One God. One of the reasons that more Jews are not converted to Christianity today is that they are sickened by the teachings that God is three."

Breanna was fascinated by all that her grandmother was telling her.

"It wasn't until over three hundred years after Christ's death that the Athanasian Creed was put into place...long after the Apostles were dead. Each one of these encyclopedias tells you pretty much how the creed got started."

"What is a creed?"

"A doctrine. A statement of belief. Pagans attempted to...and did...influence the Christian religion, especially after the death of the Apostles. When Emperor Constantine had a dream in which he saw a cross, he declared that he had become a Christian and ordered that the Christian religion be the religion of all the land...all the world that was known at that time. Everyone was forbidden to practice any other religion."

"Were all the Christian churches the same?"

"They were all one church at that time. Catholic...which means universal...was the church of all Christians. Since then, of course, people have pulled away and formed other denominations, but most of them took the doctrine of the Trinity with them and just abolished other things that were offensive to them."

"You mean like Martin Luther forming the Lutherans?"

"Yes, like that. In Constantine's day, Christians worshiped only One God. The Pagans worshiped idols and multi-gods, and it was very difficult to bring them into the Christian influence. The two groups were constantly fighting, so finally Constantine, who wanted peace between them, ordered the church to convene a conference and to come up with a doctrine that they could embrace."

Breanna listened, wide-eyed, as her grandmother continued.

"The silver craftsmen of that day were no different than those of Paul's day. Acts 19, verses 24 through 27 explain that the idol worshipers made a great deal of money crafting silver idols, and that there was a great uprising against those who worshiped one God, fearing that it would destroy their livelihoods. If they had to accept Christianity and the worship of One God, all their riches would be ruined. However, the Christian Church had been ordered to come up with something acceptable to everyone. The corruption of faith always accompanies compromise in faith. The Roman Catholic...or Christian... church created it's own multi-God...the Trinity...invented a triune God so that all the pagans had to do was to rename their Gods and continue with their silversmith businesses."

Breana sat wide-eyed. It was a lot to take in.

"How can one god be three people? It's either one god or three gods, isn't it?"

"The church was requiring all to believe this Creed of the Trinity."

"What's a creed, again?"

"A creed is a statement of faith...a statement of what the church believes. In this case, the document that spells out what they are required to believe is called the Athanasian Creed. I will give you a copy for your notebook. When you're eighty years old, you still won't understand it, but you'll have it, and it will be a reminder of what humans do to God's word. (See Addendum C)

"It's a long, drawn out document, but let me just read one part of it: 'So the Father is God, the Son God, the Holy Ghost God; yet there are not three gods but One God.'

"To me," continued her grandmother, "that says that there are three gods, but then, knowing that Christians, who believed in one God, would never accept such a concept, the Church just added the statement that there are not three gods.

"Breanna, the most important thing in your life is to know who Jesus is. We cannot believe in Him or be baptized into Him unless we know who He is. He tells us He is God's Son. God tells us that Jesus is His only begotten Son. I personally see no reason to argue with Their statements. There are not two more trustworthy persons in existence than God and Jesus. If I can't believe them, I don't want to believe anyone."

"Gammy, I think Jesus is God's Son. I don't think Jesus is God. I remember you showing me in the Bible where God said that He was the One God and that there wasn't any God before Him and that there wasn't going to be any God after Him."

"I am so pleased that we have had this opportunity to study

this subject, Breanna. Unfortunately, most young folks are members of churches that teach the Trinity, and it is so difficult to relearn once you have been led to believe a lie. You are very fortunate not to have grown up in that kind of church."

"I thought all churches taught the same thing."

"Most of them do, Breanna, but that doesn't make their teachings right or true. The Roman Catholic church was *THE* church in the beginning…the only church of the Christians. Later, some of the members broke off to establish their own denominations. However, their reasons were because of some of the things the Roman church was doing, not because of what the Roman church believed. Most took with them to their new churches, the same false doctrine of the Trinity."

"Gammy, how did you find out that the Trinity is false?"

"Well," she began with a smile, "If I'd been studying my Bible as I should have, I ought to have suspected something was wrong. In 2 Timothy, chapter 4, verse 3 we were warned that '…*the time will come when men will not listen to sound doctrine, but will add for themselves extra teachers, according to their desires, being lured by enticing words.*' Instead of studying for myself, I went to Sunday School as a child and to church as I grew up and learned all the things most churches teach. Yet, something inside me told me that some of the things they were teaching did not make sense. But I was over seventy years old before a neighbor lady invited me to go to Bible study with her."

"And she told you there was no such thing as the Trinity?"

"Well, she told me a lot more than that. However, for over seventy years I'd had this Trinity thing pounded into me, so it was not easy for me to accept what they were teaching. I use to go home after a class and get out my Bible so I could prove to them at the next class, that they were wrong. Do you know what happened?"

"What?" And she sat straight in her chair, all ears.

"I could not find a single thing that proved they were wrong. After several weeks had passed, I realized I was finding proof that they were right. Other churches were wrong."

"Is that where you learned that we don't have a soul that flies off to heaven?"

"Yes, dear, that's where."

"...and where you found out that Jesus isn't God?"

"Yes, Honey. What I really learned was that I should search out the Truth for myself. That I should get answers from the Bible and not from the church."

"But I thought you go to church."

"But I don't go to the kind of church that hires ministers to preach what they think their congregations want to hear. The men in our church all take turns giving the messages of the Bible, and none of them are paid ministers. Preaching the Gospel is what Jesus instructed us all to do; not as a profession, but as a Believer. In 1 Peter, chapter 5, verse 2, we're told what not to do...and that is to preach for money. The later translations say for dishonest gain, but the ancient documents say for money."

"But don't all preachers get paid for preaching?"

"You bet they do. In fact, some of the very large denominations pay hundreds of thousands of dollars a year to their pastors and priests. But that doesn't make it what

God wants."

"Gee, what do they live on if they don't get paid?"

"Well, the men in my church preach wonderful sermons…and teach wonderful lessons. But they have other jobs from which they make their livelihoods. Peter, if you remember, was a fisherman, yet he was one of Christ's Apostles and a wonderful preacher and teacher."

"When you are teaching me, is that the way Jesus wants the Truth to be taught?"

"Breanna, I hope I am teaching you about the Gospel of the Kingdom of God and Jesus Christ in just the way Jesus wanted us all to teach. If we find someone who doesn't know the Truth…someone who is sinning…and we don't tell them, we are responsible for that person not getting into God's Kingdom."

"The Bible says that?"

"Yes, in Ezekiel 33, verses 7 through 9, we are told that if we warn them, we have done our duty. If they do not pay attention, they will still miss out on God's kingdom, but we will not be to blame."

"Does that mean that if I know that Allison believes something that isn't true, I should tell her?"

"Yes, that's what it means."

"Wow!"

"We are not expected to convert people to the Truth if they do not want to be converted. We are expected to sow the seeds of God's word. Whether that seed falls on good soil where it can grow, causing a person to accept the Truth of God, is not our responsibility. There is a parable that describes this activity and what happens to those who do not accept the word of God."

"What's a parable, again?"

"It's a tool used in teaching that makes something more understandable. Jesus often told stories of things in life that illustrated some spiritual thing that He wanted them to understand.

"Oh, I remember. A story that means something else!"

"Yes, for instance, the parable of the sower is an example.

"In Matthew 13, verses 1 through 8, Jesus tells this story. *'Behold, a sower went out to sow. And as he sowed, some seed fell by the wayside; and the birds came and devoured them. Some fell on stony places, where they did not have much earth; and they immediately sprang up because they had no depth of earth. But when the sun was up, they were scorched, and because they had no root they withered away. And some fell among thorns, and the thorns sprang up and choked them. But others fell on good ground and yielded a good crop: some a hundredfold, some sixty, some thirty'.*"

She stopped and looked into Breanna's eyes.

"That's a parable?" Breanna asked.

"Yes. While Jesus seemed to be telling a story about a farmer sowing seeds as we think of them, that wasn't the case. He was using this story to explain something else, and if we go forward to verses 19 through 23, He explains what the story meant. He first pointed out that the seed is the Word of God, and that the seed that fell by the wayside demonstrates those that do not understand it and therefore, it is snatched away from them.

"Then, He tells us, the seed that falls on stony ground

illustrates those that hear the word of God, readily accept if with joy, but that it has no roots and does not last long. If that person faces troubles because of his faith, he loses that faith and stumbles.

"The person, He tells us, who receives the Word and let's the cares of this world and the deceitfulness of others turn them way, becomes unfruitful…of no use to Him. But, the person who accepted the Word of God; who understands it; who bears fruit…which means one who serves God…that person is illustrated by the seed that falls on good ground."

Breanna seemed fascinated by the story. Her eyes were wide and her mouth was open. "I understand now. A parable *is* a story that really means something else?"

"It's a way of using examples to teach a lesson. Yes, I guess it's a story that really means something else. This parable tells us that once we become the good ground, we are to spread the word of God to those who have not heard it…or who have heard it but do not understand it. That means we are to bear fruit."

"Gammy, I want to be good ground. I want to understand all about Jesus and about God."

"And Breanna, I believe you will." She hugged her and decided that this was enough for one day.

"Is it time for ice cream yet?" she asked.

"Sure!"

And they hurriedly gathered up their books and headed out for the ice cream parlor, where Breanna's treat was an ice cream cone consisting of chocolate, mint and strawberry piled about six inches high. Gammy could only handle one scoop of vanilla. They sat at a sidewalk table and enjoyed their treat before getting into the car.

On their way home, Gammy asked a question. "Breanna, do you now see why the Catholic church...and many others, too...might be described as apostate churches? Why they are false churches?"

"Oh, yes, Gammy. They are teaching the wrong Jesus, and they won't be able to be in God's Kingdom."

"But remember, it's not just the church, but all who believe what the church teaches. Keep in mind, the Trinity is not the only false doctrine they teach. There are many more that we haven't talked about. The Catholics teach that there is a state of being between death and going to heaven during which time loved ones can pay money and save the dead one from hell and assuring them of a place in heaven.

"And they believe that the Pope is, effectively, God and speaks for God. Catholics are required to believe everything the Pope says and are discouraged from reading the Bible."

"Why aren't they suppose to read the Bible?"

"I suspect" she answered with a smile, "because they would learn that all they are being told is false. It's everyone's duty to search the Bible for the Truth. We're not to just listen and accept whatever is fed to us from the pulpit...and God won't make an excuse for the listeners just because those who are suppose to be teaching His word, lie to them."

"And that's in the Bible, too?"

"You'll find it in Ezekiel 14, verses 9 and 10, where it tells us that the same punishment will befall those who accept the lie as those who tell the lie."

"I really need to study, don't I?"

"We all do." Gammy reached over and patted Breanna on

the knee as they pulled up in front of the small cottage that Gammy called home.

* * *

It had been a long and busy day and an early bedtime was welcome by both of them, but Breanna wanted to call her mom first. Yes, she asked about the shooting and the newsmen, but what she really wanted to do was to tell her mother who Jesus was.

# Chapter 17
# Vigilante Justice

"Hello, Michelle. I thought I'd give you a call before Breanna gets up. What is the situation with the school shooting?"

"It's really terrible. The school is closed and children are afraid to even leave their homes. Parents are acting like wild animals in front of the boy's house. I feel so sorry for his mother."

"And the boy looks so young. What ever could have entered his head? Are the newsmen still giving you fits?"

"Well, there's one outside, but this siege of the shooters house seems to have drawn them away for the most part. Because none of the children are going to school, they haven't realized that Breanna isn't here I guess, so I'm thankful for that."

"At least I'm glad they're giving you and Greg some relief."

"I'm watching the television now. I can't seem to tear myself away. The child is in court, being arraigned. They want to try him as an adult. Though he's only nine, he looks even younger…so small and helpless."

Gammy reached over and turned the TV on, turning the volume down so that it wouldn't wake Breanna.

"Oh no!"

"What is it, Michelle?" But as her own television news came into focus, she knew. Michelle gasped, then began to weep. The two women held tightly onto the receivers of their respective phones as their only way of embracing one another, but neither could speak.

The courtroom they watched was like a battlefield. Shots rang out; people were diving under tables, the suspects attorney threw himself on the boy in an attempt to protect him, taking him to the floor; the sergeant leaped over the rail in the direction of the TV camera, but it was not clear whom he was about to attack. One more shot and the sound of a scuffle off-camera.

The commentator announced that it appeared that the boy who had been accused of the school yard shooting had, himself, just been shot.

Michelle began to sob. She was watching a local program that Gammy was not able to get, but Michelle recognized the shooter. "It's Mark Abbelle, Cathy's dad."

"OH, Michelle, should I tell Breanna about this?"

"I don't know how we'll be able to keep it from her. Please, if you would."

"I'll wake her in a little bit…as soon as I can pull myself together. Maybe I'll have her get her homework done first. I wish I could think of some positive message that could come out of this, but right now, I simply can't. I'll talk to you later. I know Breanna will want to call you later anyway."

"Thanks, Mom. Bye."

A picture came on the screen of a man being restrained and led away by police. An ambulance was visible and the stretcher being carried toward its rear doors contained a patient covered from head to toe. She knew that the boy was dead.

She turned off the television and wept.

# Chapter 18
# Revenge Is Mine Sayeth The Lord

"Good morning, sleepy head."

"Hi, Gammy. It really is late, isn't it?"

"How about a nice hot cinnamon roll and some hot chocolate?"

"Mmmm, that 'ud be great!"

This had been Breanna's favorite breakfast since she was a tiny little girl and her grandmother spoiled her with it whenever she had the opportunity.

"After that, I'd like you to get your homework done and then I have a special lesson I'd like for us to study. OK?"

"Sure."

Breanna gobbled down her breakfast, and it wasn't long before she had started on her homework. While she did that, her grandmother gathered together her Bible and some pamphlets for the lesson to follow. Breanna was an excellent student, so didn't need any assistance with her homework...at least, not on this particular day. She finished quickly and put her books away...ready to join her grandmother at the dining room table.

Gammy reached across the table and gently took Breanna's

hands in her own.

"Breanna," she said softly. "I want to tell you something that happened this morning, and then I want us to see what the Bible tells us about such things. Is that all right?"

Breanna nodded. She seemed to sense an unhappy message.

"I was talking to your mom and we were both watching the news. Billy was in court when Cathy's father drew a gun and shot him. He died before they could get him to a hospital," she said softly.

Breanna was quiet. Her eyes never left her grandmother's. Huge tears rolled down her cheeks, though her expression did not change. It seemed like an eternity before either of them could speak.

"What will happen to Mr. Abbelle?" Breanna finally asked her grandmother.

"I assume he will be charged with murder. There is certainly no question but that he killed the boy."

The tears that rolled down Breanna's cheeks dropped onto her blouse, but she could not pull her eyes from her grandmother's, and she could say nothing.

"Breanna, we should never try to take the law into our own hands. It is understandable that Cathy's father would be upset and might even want to punish Billy for killing his only child, but no matter how terrible the things that might be done to us, it is not up to us to try to inflict the punishment. That is up to the courts, but more importantly, it is up to God. It is in times like this that those who study their Bibles know what they should do."

"What does the Bible say Mr. Abbelle should have done?"

she asked, wiping at her tears.

"The Bible tells us that God will bless those who refrain from rendering evil for evil…those who do not take the law into their own hands. He tells us in Romans 12, verse 19 that when evil is done to us, we are to leave the revenge…leave the punishment…to God. You've heard the saying, *'vengence is mine sayeth the Lord'*? He promises that He will execute justice for us."

"Will Mr. Abbelle go to jail?"

"We don't know that. It will all come out in a trial, but we do know that it was wrong for him to commit this act against the boy. God reserves vengeance to Himself."

"But doesn't the Bible say, 'an eye for an eye'?"

"It does. But because that might be the punishment, doesn't give us the right to inflict that punishment ourselves. Whatever the punishment that should follow any crime, it should not be done by the one who was hurt, but by God and through the courts."

"What will happen to him now?"

"He may be kept in jail till trial time, but I suspect he will probably be released after he posts bail. It takes so long these days to get to trial, I do hope he will be able to be free till then."

"Gammy, I don't think Cathy would have wanted her dad to kill Billy," Breanna said matter-of-factly.

"I'm sure she wouldn't have. Now all we can do is to pray for all those who have been so terribly hurt by this whole thing. We have to leave it all in God's hands."

"Do you think that Mr. Abbelle will go to hell for killing Billy?"

"You always have a question that sends us to the Bible. OK, get your books and let's see what you think after a lesson on hell." She smiled as Breanna went off to get her Bible.

# Chapter 19
## What and Where is Hell?

"All right, young lady, describe to me what and where you think hell is."

"Well…" and she thought for a long time. "I think it's a place in the middle of the earth. Also, there is a huge fire there and sinners go there and they burn in the fire forever."

"Where did you get the idea that such a place existed?"

She would like to have admitted to her grandmother that her Sunday School teacher told her, but she knew that her grandmother would warn her…again…against taking the teacher's word.

"I guess I thought it was in the Bible. It isn't?"

"Well, hell can certainly be in the earth, though often it is above ground. The problem is that everyone seems to have lost sight of the fact that hell is a word that means a covered place , generally a grave  or a tomb  for the dead. Since you now know that there is no Devil to rule over the hell you thought existed in the middle of the earth, maybe there just isn't such a place after all."

"Then where do sinners go?"

"Don't you remember what we said about death…that

people stay in their graves until Christ comes?"

"Yes, I remember, but those that aren't going to be in God's Kingdom must go somewhere!"

"How about back to the grave...to a second death...an eternal death?"

Breanna thought about this for a minute before speaking.

"They perish!" Suddenly she understood John 3, verse 16 which told her that God so loved the world that He gave His only begotten Son, that whosoever believed in Him should not perish. She realized that that verse had said that if you didn't believe in Jesus, to perish was the punishment. Jesus didn't come to add an additional punishment for those who rejected Him...the punishment for such rejection had been established in the beginning...when Adam and Eve disobeyed God.

"That's right," her grandmother responded. "You only need to go to 2 Thessalonians, chapter 1, verse 9 to have it spelled out clearly. Those who know not God and those who do not acknowledge the Gospel of Jesus Christ, shall be rewarded with *'everlasting destruction'*, not everlasting *burning*. It is the destruction...the perishing...that lasts forever, not the fire."

"Where did these ideas of a burning hell come from, Gammy?" Breanna clearly was disturbed at the things she had been taught.

"Words like hell, sheol, hades and gehenna have been used to described the abode of the sinful dead. However, each of these words has a meaning that is far from the description of an eternal fiery jumping-off place for sinners."

Breanna stared at her grandmother, waiting for her to

explain further…and she did.

"The teaching, that at death those who are wicked go to a place of eternal suffering, torment and misery…burning through all of eternity…is contradicted throughout the Bible. Using scare tactics to get converts, clergy has, for decades, supported these teachings by misreading the passages about fire. Nothing can burn forever without being completely consumed. The fire spoken of in the Bible has now been generally accepted as a description of God's judgment.

"Deuteronomy 4, verse 24 tells us this when it says, '*For the Lord, your God, is a consuming fire*'; and Hebrews 12, verse 29 tells us the same thing…that '*Our God is a consuming fire*'. And there are several verses that tell us what happens to man after death. You may want to jot them down."

Breanna took a pencil and paper while her grandmother opened her Bible and began to read.

"From Psalm 37 verse 20, '*The wicked shall perish…they shall vanish away*'; from 2 Thessalonians 1 verse 9, '*They shall be punished with everlasting destruction*'. It's the destruction that is everlasting, not the punishment; then in Psalm 49 verse 14, '*Like sheep they are laid in the grave; death shall feed on them…and their beauty shall be consumed in the grave*'."

"They just turn to dust, Gammy?"

"We all will. But those that '*receive not the love of the Truth that they might be saved*' will not be resurrected and given immortal bodies. While they may get a glimpse of God's Kingdom so that they know what they have missed, their destiny is a second death…one that is everlasting. They will never enjoy the Kingdom of God. A popular Scripture used by those believing and teaching the fiery hell of torment, torture and eternal burning is Matthew 18 verse 8. *'And if thy hand offend thee, cut it off, it is better for thee to enter into life lame or maimed, rather than having two hands or two feet, to be cast into the everlasting fire.'"*

"Doesn't that say they will burn forever?"

"It says that the fire will burn forever, not that the sinner will burn forever."

It was obvious that Breanna could not understand the difference.

"The word hell of this Scripture is the word 'gehenna', and does refer to a specific location, but it isn't in the center of the earth were sinners are sent to burn forever. Gehenna was a place just on the outskirts of Jerusalem, where garbage was burned, and where the bodies of unclaimed dead and criminals were thrown to be consumed…to be destroyed. It was kept burning all the time for sanitary reasons. Ministers picked up on this Scripture and used it in their hell-fire-and-damnation sermons to frighten people into joining the church, telling them that they would suffer burning forever if they did not."

"Oooh, that's scary."

"That was the whole idea. I don't think you hear much of that any more, though many pastors still believe…and teach…that hell is a place of fire, in the center of the earth, where the Devil reigns."

"I think that's dishonest, Gammy, don't you?"

"I certainly do. The Bible is so full of wonderful, true messages that are full of hope for eternal life. Those are the promising messages they should be conveying, not trying to scare their congregations."

"I'm so glad to know about the Kingdom, and I really will try hard to live my life like Jesus wants me to, Gammy."

"I'm sure you'll succeed, Honey. Now your question that started us out on this study was whether I thought Mr. Abbelle would go to hell for killing Billy. What do you think, now?"

Breanna looked at her grandmother, but said nothing for what seemed like minutes. When she finally spoke, it was with a question. "Mr. Abbelle will stay dead forever, won't he? He won't be able to get into God's Kingdom, will he?"

"We don't know that."

"But if the court says he's guilty of murder…"

"That only condemns him in the eyes of the world. It has nothing to do with God's Kingdom, and doesn't mean that God won't forgive him if he repents and asks for forgiveness."

"God will forgive people, even if they kill somebody?" She seemed genuinely surprised at the thought.

"There is nothing anyone can do that is so bad that God will not forgive it if they are truly sorry and ask for His forgiveness."

"WOW!"

"I expect that Mr. Abbelle was sorry for his actions as soon as he pulled the trigger. Having lost Cathy, he certainly knows how it feels to lose a child, and I feel sure that as soon as he has an opportunity to reflect on how Billy's mother feels, his heart will ache."

"I bet he's awfully sorry right now." Breanna seemed sad

herself, at the thought.

"I'm sure he is, and all you and I can do for him is to pray that he will be able to ask for and receive God's forgiveness."

"Tonight, when I say my prayers, I'm going to ask God to forgive him."

"And so will I, Breanna."

# Chapter 20
# It's All Over

"Hello," she answered breathlessly.

They had heard the phone as they reached the garage, and Gammy had run to get it before the answering machine picked up.

"Hi, Mom. It's Michelle."

"Yes, dear. Excuse my breathlessness but Breanna and I have just gotten back from a visit to the juice mart and I had to run to get the phone. I'm not as young as I use to be." She laughed.

"Do you want to take a minute to catch your breath?"

"No, no, I'm fine. How are things there?"

"Bad news and good news, Mom. The bad first. Mr. Abbelle was indicted this morning. They charged him with murder then let him out without bail until the trial. A few hours later, his wife found his body in their basement. He'd shot himself."

"Oh, Michelle, I'm so sorry to hear that. I know he must have been terribly tormented by what he did to the boy."

"The newscasters are saying that he left three notes. One to his wife, one to his pastor and one to the boy's mother. Of course, they aren't saying what was in them."

"I hope that he asked for forgiveness and that it will be granted. I feel so sorry for his wife. I believe Breanna told me that she has no other family."

"I believe that's true."

"What's the good news? After that, I could use some good news."

"Well, since there seems to be no reason for Breanna to stay away, maybe she'd better come home and get back to school."

"That may be good news for you, but it doesn't sound so good to me." They both laughed, but both knew Michelle was right.

"It's Friday," said Gammy. "Why don't I keep her until Sunday. If there's any Bible subjects she's inquisitive about, I'd like to clear them up for her. I'll put her on a plane early Sunday morning so she'll be there in time to get a good nights sleep before she has to go to school on Monday. Will that suit you?"

"That's great, Mom. I'm at work right now, so I won't talk to her this time. Give her a kiss for me and tell her I'm looking forward to getting her back."

"I will Michelle, and thank you for sharing her with me. She is a very special young lady."

\* \* \*

"Honey, since you're going home of Sunday, I thought we'd spend Saturday doing some of the things you'd enjoy doing and covering any Bible subjects you'd like. OK?"

"Great! Can we go to the lake and feed the ducks?"

"You bet! We'll take a picnic lunch and spend the day."

"Maybe we could take our Bibles along…I do have a question."

"That sounds pretty good…like killing two birds with one stone…at least doing two things in one place. You're on!"

They both chuckled and Gammy suggested to Breanna that she might want to get completely caught up on her homework today, so she'd be up to the minute when she went back to school but would be free all day Saturday to play. Breanna thought that was a wonderful idea and headed gleefully to her room to get that project taken care of.

She had enjoyed her visit with her grandmother and would have been happy to stay another week or so. But now that she knew she was going home in less than two days, she realized how much she had missed her mom and dad, and was happy to be going home.

# Chapter 21
# Who is Lucifer?

Saturday morning they were both up early. Gammy was preparing a lunch for their trip to the lake and Breanna was getting her clothes together so that packing to go home would be an easy chore when she got back from the lake. When she had done all she felt she could do at the moment, she skipped into the kitchen and peered into the picnic basket to see what was for lunch. She was pleased. They headed off to the lake and their last day of fun together until summer, when Breanna would be back.

They spread the huge beach towel on the grass, placed the picnic basket in the center, and opened the low folding chairs they'd brought for comfort. Breanna would have no trouble getting in and out of hers, but her grandmother wondered if she'd ever get up once she got in one of them. While she was lowering herself into the chair, Breanna was already digging into the lunch basket, searching for the bread crumbs she'd brought for the ducks.

"Oh Gammy, look!"

Following the direction of Breanna's pointing finger, Gammy saw a mother duck being followed across the grass by five tiny ducklings. Breanna was ecstatic! Gammy took out her throw-away camera and got wonderful shots of Breanna's happy face as she knelt to watch the little duck family waddle to and fro. Coming to the lake had been an excellent choice of things to do and, until lunch time, Breanna was happy feeding not only the mother and five ducklings, but the other dozen ducks that gathered around for a handout. In fact, they might not have had an opportunity to *eat* lunch if the bread crumbs had not run out.

Breanna had her favorite peanut butter, spread with sweet pickle relish and her grandmother enjoyed a tuna fish salad. When they had finished off the sandwiches and the diet pops, there was an array of fruits from which to choose…and Breanna chose one of each. Her grandmother ate an apple. With their tummies full, Gammy wondered aloud if they were up to Bible study

"Oh, yes, Gammy. I'm leaving tomorrow and I do have a question."

"OK, shoot."

"Well, I've been studying the lesson you gave me on the Devil and you didn't say anything about Lucifer. I looked it up in the Bible dictionary and it said that Lucifer was a name for the Devil."

"That's what they teach all right! But I think you're going to find, when you search the Bible that Lucifer isn't the Devil, especially since you already know that there is no such thing as a devil-person as most believe. I don't know how I could have forgotten to tell you about Lucifer." And she laughed as she reached for her Bible.

Breanna settled comfortably in her beach chair, waiting for

the story of the fallen angel.

"If you had your Concordance with you…"

"I do, Gammy," she exclaimed as she reached into her backpack and pulled out both the Concordance and her Bible.

"Well, then, look up Lucifer, and you'll see that it appears only one place in the Bible."

By now Breanna had found it and informed her grandmother that the word appeared in the book of Isaiah, chapter 14 verse 12.

"*'How you are fallen from heaven, O Lucifer, son of the morning. How you are cut down to the ground, you who weakened the nations,*' her grandmother read, "but in order to understand even that one verse, you need to know something else. The fact that the Bible often uses heavenly language to describe worldly things."

"Like a parable?"

"Well, not exactly, but very similar. Throughout the Bible, the use of the word heaven is often used to mean people in high places, like kings or rulers of governments…and sometimes even referring to governments themselves. The word earth will mean the people of those governments or kingdoms."

"So what does this verse mean?"

"First, let's see what the word Lucifer means. I have quoted the passage from your Bible, the New King James Version. If you look in my Bible, it reads differently," and she read:

"*'How have you falled from heaven! Howl in the morning for you have fallen down to the ground, O reviler of the nations."*

"But Gammy, that doesn't say anything about Lucifer."

"It really does. Lucifer means day star or morning star, and this verse is symbolic of the King of Babylon...not an evil devil-person. If you have ever seen a morning star, you know that it is bright in the sky but for a very short time, then is gone as quickly as it appeared. God was telling Isaiah to tell the King of Babylon that that is what he was...a bright star that would fall because he had failed to give God credit for his rise, and because he considered himself as powerful as God."

"How do you know all that, Gammy?"

"By reading more than one verse of the Bible," she said emphatically, a reminder to Breanna that she had told her this over and over before. "The word Lucifer is from a Latin word meaning light bearing. The original Hebrew word means bright star or morning star. We only have to go back a few verses...back to verse 4...and it should become perfectly clear that God was telling Isaiah to give the King of Babylon a message about the errors he'd made. This King had thought that he had risen to his high status all by himself. The King had given God no credit for his success."

Breanna looked at verse 4 and sure enough, it was God telling Isaiah to give the message to the King of Babylon.

"So Lucifer was the King of Babylon?"

"Symbolically, yes. The evil King who would be brought down because of his arrogance. I believe that the Amplified Bible translates the verse in an even clearer way. *'How have you fallen from heaven. O light bringer and day star, son of the morning! How you have been cut down to the ground, you who weakened and laid low the nations. (O blasphemous, satanic king of Babylon!)'"*

After reading verses 4 through 13, Breanna asked a question. "Did God really do all those things to the King?"

"Yes, he did."

"Gee, how do you know that?"

"Because the King had gotten the same warning from the prophet Daniel. In that prophesy, instead of the King being symbolized as a falling star, he was presented as a tree that had grown into the heavens and was cut down. But God told Daniel to tell the King that the roots of the tree would be left."

"What chapter is that in?"

"That story is told in the 4th chapter of Daniel."

Breanna flipped the pages till she came to the book of Daniel and found the 4th chapter.

"Go to verse 10 and you'll see that the King is telling Daniel what his dream was. Then when you get to verse 14, he begins to tell him the part that he doesn't understand."

Breanna read to herself as her grandmother watched with interest. She could see, from the scowl on Breanna's face, that she didn't really understand that what she read had anything to do with Lucifer.

"In these verses, Honey, the tree that had grown to heaven was the symbol of the king of Babylon, while the Isaiah verses used a falling star...Lucifer. Both mean the same thing. This King had become great, had risen to the heights, overtaking nations, and considering himself above God. Again, the same message that his arrogance was unacceptable to God."

Breanna, like so many young folks, could listen and read at the same time, so she was already at verse 15 with a question.

"Does the order to cut down the tree mean the same thing as the falling star?"

"It does. Lucifer, or the morning star was felled by God, just as this tree of Daniel was cut down. In both cases, we are talking about the King of Babylon. If you go to verse 24, Daniel begins to tell the King the interpretation of his dream." Both looked at their Bibles and read.

Breanna still had a question about verse 15.

"What does God mean by leaving the stump and the root?"

"That is a wonderful message, Breanna. I'm glad you didn't miss it. That tells us that God will always forgive us for our wrongs. He is leaving open the possibility that the king will repent and that this tree, which represents him, will grow again. In fact, the statement, *'till you know that the Most High rules in the kingdom of men and gives it to whomever he chooses'*, seems to say that He expects the King to repent."

"It does?" Breanna didn't see it.

"He says, *'till you know'*…not *'if you learn'*.

"Did God actually make him like an animal, grazing on grass and with claws?"

"He did, indeed. The king lost his mind and grazed like an animal. His hair grew wild and his nails grew to look like claws. He did more than that. For seven years, the King was like a wild beast. Grazing outside the gates of the kingdom. Then, after seven years, he raised his eyes to heaven, his understanding returned to him, and he blessed God…and his kingdom was returned to him. He praised God and knew that God really was in control. Now, tell me who Lucifer was."

"He was the King of Babylon…and the tall tree was the

King of Babylon, too."

"And both show that he was taken down because of the King's arrogance and pride...because he did not give God the credit for his rise."

"God gives us everything we have, doesn't He?" Breanna asked with gentle affection in her voice.

"He does...and we need to always remember that, and to thank Him for all the good things we have in our lives."

"I thank Him for letting me come stay with you so I could learn more about Him," Breanna said as she moved over to give her grandmother a hug.

"It has been a real blessing to me, too, Breanna. You have made these past few days some of the happiest of my life." She kissed her grandaughter and suggested they say goodbye to the ducks that had wandered some distance away, and to get ready to leave.

It had been a nice, albeit long, day and they needed to get home and get Breanna ready for her trip home.

# Chapter 22
# Time To Go Home

She put Breanna's suitcase down by the seats that faced the runway so they could watch the planes come and go.

"Breanna, there are a few things I want you to remember above all else…things I want you to take with you in your heart. One, that God's word is Truth and we can never enter His Kingdom if we believe in false doctrines."

After a long silence, Breanna spoke. "Gammy, doesn't incarnate mean to change to a different person?"

"Yes, to change the form of a thing. To make one thing into the form of another. That's what it means, but what does that have to do with Jesus?"

"Well, isn't Jesus God incarnate?"

"Is He? Did you find that in the Bible?"

"I know! I'm not suppose to take anyone's word for things, and that I'm suppose to look it up in the Bible…"

"And did you?"

"I tried to look up the word in my Concordance and I couldn't find it, so I don't know any other way to look it up in the Bible."

"Well, little girl, if it isn't in your Concordance, you can be pretty sure it isn't in your Bible!"

Her grandmother could almost see the wheels turning in the child's head.

"The Bible tells us that Jesus was a manifestation of his Father...that He was a revelation of God...*NOT* that He was the incarnation of God."

"What is the difference, Gammy?"

"*To be God's manifestation* means that Jesus came to manifest to us, or to show us, God's purpose, not that He came to *be* God. And likewise, a revelation means just what it says, that Jesus came to reveal God and His purpose.

"God has revealed Himself in many ways, starting with the creation of the world and of man. You cannot look at this world, with its beauty and the intricate design of human beings, and not know how wonderful God is...not see his power and goodness. It tells us so much about God. The more scientists learn, and tell us, the more marvelous God's creation seems...so His creation is still speaking to us...still manifesting Him. And Psalm 19, verses 1 and 2 tell us that the heavens declare the glory of God; that the day utters God's word and the night shows His knowledge. God is still declaring Himself through the fabulous heavens, about which we are learning more and more of His wonder every day.

"Then, in another way, he made Himself known through His laws...through the Ten Commandments that He delivered through Moses and which are spelled out in the first 16 verses of the 20$^{th}$ chapter of Exodus.

"He revealed Himself through His prophets (Hebrews 1:1) and His infallible words were recorded by those He chose as His prophets, creating the Scriptures of the Old Testament.

But the greatest of God's manifestations was His own Son, Jesus, whom He sent for that very purpose.

"It says that Jesus was sent to manifest God?"

"Romans 9:17 tells us that Jesus came to *declare* God."

"So God used all those ways to tell people about Himself?"

"Honey, He didn't stop at that. After Jesus died, the Apostles continued to teach about God and His Son; They, and others, wrote the messages that were later compiled to form the New Testament, which, then, is another manifestation of God and Jesus... and guess what?"

"What?"

"He is still being declared...being manifested...being explained...by those who love Him, believe in His Son, and teach others."

"So Jesus just came to *tell us* about God, not to *be* God?"

"John 1, verse 18, tells us that no one has seen God, but that Jesus came to declare Him. Yes, to *tell us* about Him, and to assure us, that if we believe that He is God's Son, and accept Him as our Savior, we can *be* in God's Kingdom for eternity.

"Boy, I sure have a lot to learn, don't I, Gammy?"

"We never stop learning, Honey, if we really want to know the Truth."

"I promise I'll study a lot, Gammy."

"I'm sure you will, and I know that the more you study, the more fascinated you'll become with the Bible. I know I did. It's time for your plane, but there is one more important thing I want you to be sure to remember. We will not be excused for believing a lie just because a preacher tells us its true.

We're given the responsibility of studying the Scriptures for ourselves and in searching out its messages."

"But it's so hard, Gammy."

"It will get easier as you keep at it…and I can already tell that you are going to be a wonderful Bible student."

"I hope so. I'll try, really I will."

"You already know that most churches teach false lessons about the most important thing…the thing we need most to know if we are to have salvation."

"Like who Jesus is?"

"Like who Jesus is! Don't ever forget that He is God's Son. You can become God's daughter by becoming Jesus' sister when you accept Him as your savior, are baptized in His name, and follow His commandments throughout your life."

"I want to, Gammy. I really want to." She threw her arms around her grandmother's neck and they enjoyed a final embrace just as Breanna's plane was announced.

They kissed goodbye and the same pretty attendant that had brought her off the plane on her arrival, led her aboard as she waved to her grandmother with one hand and wiped her tears away with the other.

Gammy, wiping away her own tears, stood until the plane left the ground, waving just in case Breanna could see her.

# Addendum A

Soul as is explained in *Encyclopedia Britanica*. The "soul" is the functioning unit of an individual, not some part of him"….in other words, it continues, the soul is "the living, mortal person and not a homesick visitor from the eternal region." But we need only to compare the various translations of the *Bible* to get the meaning of "soul". The Bible defines itself, if we truly seek the definition.

King James Version shown by (KJ)
New King James Version by (NKJ)
Lamsa (language spoken by Jesus) by (L)
New International Version by (NIV)
Modern Language (M)
Living Bible (LV)
Revised Standard (RV)

"…and man became a *living soul*." (KJ, M)
"…and man became a *living being*."(L,
 NKJ, NIV, RV)
"…and man became a *living person*…(LV)
(Genesis 2:7)

"...and *my soul* shall live because of thee."
(KJ)
"... and that *I* may live because of you..."
(NKJ)
"...and *my life* shall be spared because of
you." (L, NIV, M, RV)
"...and spare *my life*..." (LV)
(Genesis 12:13)


"...that *soul* shall be cut off from his
people..." (KJ)
"...that *person* shall be cut off from his
people..." (NKJ, L, RV)
"...any...*male*...shall be cut off from his
people..." (NIV)
"...that *person* shall be eliminated..." (M)
"...*anyone*...shall be cut off from his
people..." (LV)
(Genesis 17:14)


"...and *my soul* shall live." (KJ, NKJ)
"...*my life* will be spared." (L, NIV))
"...to save *my life*..." (M)
"...and *my life* will be saved..." (LV, RV)
(Genesis 19:20)


"...that *my soul* shall bless thee before I
die." (KJ, L)
"...that *my soul* may bless you..." (NKJ)

"…that *I* may give you my blessing before I die." (NIV, M, LV)
"…that *I* may bless you before I die…"
(RV)
(Genesis 27:4)

"…that *your soul* may bless me." (KJ, L, NKJ)
"…so that *you* may give me your blessing."
(NIV)
"…so that *yourself* may heartily bless me…" (M)
"…so that *you* will bless me…" (LV)
"…that *you* may bless me…" (RV)
(Genesis 27:19)

"…that *my soul* shall bless thee…" (KJ, L)
"…that *my soul* may bless you…" (NKJ)
"…that *I* may give you my blessing." (NIV)
"…so *I* may personally bless you…" (M)
"…*I* will…bless you with all my heart…"
(LV)
"…that *I* may eat…and bless you…" (RV)
(Genesis 27:25)

"…so that *thy soul* may bless me…" (KJ, L)
"…that *your soul* may bless me…" (NKJ)
"…so that *you* may give me your blessing."
(NIV)
"…so that *you* may personally bless me…"

(M)
"…so that *you* can give me your finest blessing…" (LV)
"…that *you* may bless me…" (RV)
(Genesis 27:31)

"…And his *soul* clave unto Dinah…" (KJ)
"…his *soul* was strongly attracted to Dinah…" (NKJ)
"…And his *soul* longed for Dinah…" (L)
"…His *heart* was drawn to Dinah…" (NIV)
"…*He* was passionately in love with Dinah…" (M)
"…*He* fell deeply in love with her…" (LV)
"…and *his soul* was drawn to Dinah…" (RV)
(Genesis 34:3)

"…the *soul* of my son…" (KJ, L, NKJ, RV)
"…*my son* has his heart set…(NIV)
"…*my son* affections…after your daughter…" (M)
"…*my son* is truly in love with your daughter…" (LV)
(Genesis 34:8)

"…as *her soul was departing*…" (KJ, L, NKJ, RV)
"…as *she was dying*…" (NIV)
"…for *she expired*…" (M)

"…and with *Rachel's last breath*…" (LV)
(Genesis 35:18)


"…we saw the anguish of *his soul*…" (KJ,
L, NKJ)
"…we knew how distressed *he* was…"
(NIV, RV)
"…the agony of his soul…" (M)
"…we saw his terror and anguish…" (LV)
(Genesis 42:21)


"…let not my *soul* enter their council…"
(NKJ)
"…O my *soul*, come not into their
secrets…" (KJ)
"…*I* did not agree to sit in their counsels..."
(L)
"…let *me* not enter into their council…"
(NIV)
"…my soul, do not share in their plot…"
(M)
"…O my soul, stay away from them…"
(LV)
"…O my soul, come not into their
counsel…" (RV)
(Geneis 49:6)


"…that *soul* shall be cut off from Israel…"
(KJ)
"…that *person* shall be cut off from

Israel…" (NKJ, RV)
"…that *person* shall perish from Israel…"
(L)
"…*whoever* eats…must be cut off from
Israel…" (NIV)
"…that *person* shall be eliminated from
Israel…" (M)
"…*anyone*…shall be excommunicated from
Israel…" (LV)
 (Exodus 12:15)


"…even that *soul* shall be cut off…" (KJ)
"…that *person* shall be cut off…" (NKJ,
RV)
"…that *person* shall perish…" (L)
"…*whoever* eats…must be cut off…" (NIV)
"…*anyone*…shall be excommunicated…"
(M, LV)
 (Exodus 12:19)


"…a ransom for *his soul*…" (KJ, LVV)
"…a ransom for *himself*…" (NKJ, L, RV)
"…a ransom for *his life*…" (NIV, M)
(Exodus 30:12)


"…that *soul* shall be cut off…" (KJ, RV)
"…that *person* shall be cut off…" (NKJ)
"…that *soul* shall surely be cut off…" (L)
"…*whoever*…must be cut off…" (NIV)
"…that person shall be eliminated…" (M)

160

"...anyone...shall be killed..." (LV)
(Exodus 31:14)

"...if *a soul* shall sin..." (KJ, RV)
"...if *anyone* sins..." (NKJ, M)
"...if *a person* shall sin..." (L)
"...if the anointed *priest* sins..." (NIV)
"...*anyone*...who breaks any of my
commandments..." (LV)
(Leviticus 4:2; 5:1)

"...if a *soul* touch any unclean thing..."
(KJ)
"...if a *person* touches any unclean
thing...(NKJ)
"...if any *person* touches any unclean
thing...(L)
"...if a *person* touches anything..." (NIV)
"...when a *person* contacts an unclean
thing..." (M)
"...*anyone* touching anything...unclean..."
(LV)
"...if *anyone* touches an unclean thing..."
(RV)
(Leviticus 5:2)

"...if a *soul* swear..." (KJ)
"...if a *person* swears..." (NKJ)
"...if any *person* swears...(L)
"...if a *person*...takes an oath..." (NIV)

"...if a *person* unthinkingly utters an oath..." (M)
"...if *anyone* makes a rash vow..." (LV)
"...if *anyone* utters...a rash oath..." (RV)
(Leviticus 5:4)

"...if a *soul* commit a trespass..." (KJ)
"...if a *person* commits a trespass..." (NKKJ)
"...if any *person* commits a trespass..." (L)
"...when a *person* commits a violation..." (NIV)
"...when a *person* behaves unfaithfully..." (M)
"...if *anyone* sins..." (LV)
"...if *anyone* commits a breach of faith..." (RV)
(Leviticus 5:15)

"...if a *soul* sin..." (KJ, )
"...if a *person* sins..." (NKJ, NIV, M)
"...if any *person* sins..." (L)
"...*anyone* who disobeys..." (LV)
"...if *anyone* sins..." (RV)
(Leviticus 5:17; 6:2)

"...and the *soul* that eateth..." (KJ)
"...and the *person* who eats of it..." (NKJ, L, M)
"...and the *person* who eats any of it..."

(NIV)
"… and the *priest* who eats it…" (LV)
"…and *he* who eats it…" (RV)
(Leviticus 7:18)

"…that *soul* shall be cut off…" (KJ)
"…that *person* shall be cut off…" (NKJ, L, NIV, RV)
"…that person shall be eliminated…" (M)
"…the priest…shall be cut off…" (LV)
(Leviticus 7:20)

"…the *soul* that touch any unclean thing…" (KJ)
"…the *person* who touches any unclean thing…" (NKJ)
"…the *person* that shall touch any unclean thing…" (L)
"…if *anyone* touches anything unclean…" (NIV)
"…the *person* who contacts anything unclean…" (M)
"…*anyone* who touches anything… unclean…" (LV)
"…if *anyone* touches an unclean things…" (RV)
(Leviticus 7:21)

"…that *soul* that eateth it…" (KJ)
"…the *person* who eats it…" (NKJ)

"…the *person* that eats it…" (L)
"…*anyone* who eats the fat…" (NIV)
"…*whoever* eats...shall be eliminated…"
(M)
"…*anyone* who eats…shall be outlawed…"
(LV)
"…*every person* shall be cut off…" (RV)
(Leviticus 7:25)

"…whatsoever *soul* it be that eateth any
manor of blood…" (KJ)
 "…*whoever* eats any blood…" (NKJ, RV)
 "…*whosoever* eats any manor of blood…"
(L)
"…if *anyone* eats blood…" (NIV)
"…the *person* who eats any blood…" (M)
"…*anyone* who does (eat blood)…" (LV)
(Leviticus 7:27)

"…that *soul* shall be cut off…" (KJ)
"…that *person* shall be cut off…" (NKJ,
RV)
"…the *person* that eats it shall be cut off…"
(L)
"…that *person* must be cut off…" (NIV)
"…that *person* shall be eliminated…" (M)
"…*anyone*…shall be excommunicated…"
(LV)
(Leviticus 7:27)

"…that *soul* that eateth blood…" (KJ)
"…that *person* who eats blood…" (NKJ, L, NIV)

"…every *man*…and every *immigrant*…who eats blood…" (M)
"…*anyone*…who eats blood…"(LV)
"…any *man*…or any *stranger*…who eats blood…" (RV)
(Leviticus 17:10)

"…to make an atonement for your *souls*…" (KJ, NKJ, M, LV, RV)
"…to make an atonement for *yourselves*…" (L, NIV)
(Leviticus 17:11)

"…*no soul* of you shall eat blood…" (KJ)
"…*no one* among you shall eat blood…" (NKJ)
"…*no person*…shall eat blood…" (L)
"…*none of you* shall eat blood…" (NIV, M)
"…*none of you* may eat blood…" (LV)
"…*no person* among you shall eat blood…" (RV)
(Leviticus 17:12)

"…and every *soul* that eateth…" (KJ)
"…and every *person* who eats…" (NKJ, L, M)

"…*anyone*…who eats…" (NIV)
"…and *everyone* who eats…" (LV)
"…and every *person* that eats…" (RV)
(Leviticus 17:15

"…and *the soul* that turneth after…" (KJ)
"…and *the person* who turns to…" (NKJ, M)
"…and *the person* who goes after…" (L)
"…*the person* who turns…" (NIV)
"…*anyone* who consults…" (LV)
"…if *a person* turns…" (RV)
(Leviticus 20:6)

"…I will set My face against that *soul*…" (KJ)
"…I will set My face against that *person*…" (NKJ, RV)
"…I will pour out My anger against that *person*…" (L)
"…I will cut *him* off…" (NIV)
"…I will eliminate *him*…" (M)
"…I will cut that *person* off…" (LV)
(Leviticus 20:6)

"…that *soul* shall be cut off…" (KJ)
"…that *person* shall be cut off…" (NKJ, L, RV)
"…that *person* must be cut off…" (NIV)
"…that *person* will be removed…" (M)

"…*he* shall be discharged…" (LV)
(Leviticus 22:3)

"…the *soul* which hath touched…" (KJ)
"…the *person* who has touched…" (NKJ)
"…any *person* who touches…" (L, RV)
"…the *one* who touches…" (NIV, M)
"…any priest who touches…" (LV)
(Leviticus 22:5-6)

"…if the priest buys any *soul*…" (KJ)
"…if the priest buys a *person*…" (NKJ)
"…if a priest buys any *person*…" (L)
"…if a priest buys a *slave*…" (NIV,LV, RV)
"…a *person* whom the priest buys…" (M)
(Leviticus 22:11)

"…for whosoever *soul* it be that shall not be afflicted…" (KJ)
"…for any *person* who is not afflicted in *soul*…" (NKJ)
"…for whatever *person* it be who does not humble *himself*…" (L)
"…*anyone* who does not deny *himself*…" (NIV)
"…*whoever* does not humble *himself*…" (M)
"…*anyone* who does not spend the day is repentance…" (LV)
"…*whoever* is not afflicted…" (RV)

(Leviticus 23:29)

"…whatsoever *soul* it be that doeth any work…" (KJ)

"…and any *person* who does any work…" (NKJ)

"…and whatever *person* it be who does any work…" (L)

"…*anyone* who does any work on that day…" (NIV, M, LV)

"…*whoever* does any work…" (RV)

(Leviticus 23:30)

"…and the same *soul* will I destroy…" (KJ)

"…that *person* I will destroy…" (NKJ, M)

"…the same *person* will I destroy…" (L, RV)

"…I will destroy *anyone*…" (NIV)

"…and I will put to death *anyone*…" (LV)

(Leviticus 23:30)

"…and My *soul* shall not abhor you…" (KJ, NKJ, L, RV)

"…and *I* will not abhor you…" (NIV)

"…my *soul* will not reject you…" (M)

"…*I*…will not despise you…" (LV)

(Leviticus 26:11)

"…if your *soul* abhor my judgments…" (KJ)

"…if *you* despise my statutes…" (NKJ)

"...if *you* despise my laws..." (L, M)
"...if *you* reject my decrees..." (NIV)
"...but (*you*) reject my laws..." (LV)
"...if *you* spurn my statutes..." (RV)
(Leviticus 26:15)

"...and *My soul* shall abhor you..." (KJ, NKJ, L, RV)
"...and *I* will abhor you..." (NIV, LV)
"...my soul shall loathe you..." (M)
(Leviticus 26:30)

"...because their *souls* abhorred My statutes..." (KJ, NKJ, L, RV)
"...because *they* have abhorred My judgments..."(NIV)
"...because their souls abhorred my laws..." (M)
"...(they) shall accept their punishment for rejecting my laws..."(LV)
(Leviticus 26:43)

"...even the same *soul*..." (KJ)
"...that same *person*..." (NKJ)
"...that *person*..." (L, RV)
"...that *man*..." (NIV)
"...if any individual..."(M)
"...anyone...shall be..." (LV)
(Numbers 9:13)

"...our *soul* is dried away..." (KJ)
"...our *whole being* is dried up..." (NKJ)
"...our soul is dried up..." (L)
"...*we* have lost our appetite..." (NIV)
"...our *souls* are famished..." (M)
"...our *strength* is gone..." (LV)
"...our *strength* is dried up..." (RV)
(Numbers 11:6)

"...if any *soul* sin..." (KJ)
"...if a *person* sins..." (NKJ, L)
"...if just one *person* sins..." (NIV, M)
"...a single *individual*..." (LV)
"...if one *person*..." (RV)
(Numbers 15:27)

"...atonement for *the soul*..." (KJ)
"...atonement for *the person*..." (NKJ, L, M, RV)
"...atonement...for *the one* who erred..."
"...atonement for him..." (LV)
(Numbers 15:28)

"...the *soul* that doeth..." (KJ)
"...the *person*..." (NKJ, M, RV)
"...the *person* who..." (L)
"...*anyone* who..." (NIV, LV)
(Numbers 15:30)

"…*that soul* shall be cut off…" (KJ)
"…*he* shall be cut off…" (NKJ)
"…*that person* shall be cut off…" (L)
"…*that person* must be cut off…" (NIV)
"…*that person* must be destroyed…" (M)
"…*anyone*…shall be cut off…" (LV, RV)
(Numbers 15:30)

"…that *soul* shall utterly be cut off…" (KJ)
"…that *person* shall be completely cut off…" (NKJ)
"…that *person* shall utterly be cut off…" (L, RV)
"…that *person* must surely be cut off…" (NIV)
"…*that person* must unquestionably be cut off…" (M)
"…*he* must be executed…" (LV)
(Numbers 15:31)

"…that *soul* shall be cut off…" (KJ)
"…that *person* shall be cut off…" (NKJ, L, RV)
"…that *person* must be cut off…" (NIV)
"…that *person* must be excommunicated…" (M, LV)
(Numbers 19:13)

"…that *soul* shall be cut off…" (KJ, L)
"…that *person* shall be cut off…" (NKJ,

RV)

"...*he* must be cut off..." (NIV)

"...that *person* must be excommunicated..." (M, LV)

(Numbers 19:20)


"...and the *soul* that toucheth it..." (KJ)

"...and the *person* who touches it..." (NKJ, L)

"...and *anyone* who touches it..." (NIV)

"...the unclean *person* touches..." (M, RV)

"...the defiled *person* touches..." (LV)

(Numbers 19:22)


"...and the *soul* of the people..." (KJ, NKJ)

"...the *people*..." (L, LV, RV)

"...but the *people*..." (NIV)

"...the *people*, however..." (M)

(Numbers 21:4)


"...*our soul* loatheth this light bread..." (KJ)

"...*our soul* loaths this worthless bread..." (NKJ)

"...*our soul* is weary with this inferior bread..." (L)

"...*we* detest this miserable food..." (NIV)

"...*we* loath to our souls..." (M)

"...*we* hate this insipid manna..." (LV)

"...*we* loath this worthless food..." (RV)

(Numbers 21:5)

"…an oath to bind *his soul* with a bond…"
(KJ)
"…swears an oath to bind *himself*…" (NKJ,
L)
"…takes an oath to obligate *himself*…"
(NIV)
"…a *man*…takes *an oath* to abstain from
something…" (M)
"…*anyone*…*a promise* to the Lord…" (LV)
"…a *man vows* to the Lord…" (RV)
(Numbers 30:2)

"…wherewith she hath bound her *soul*.."
(KJ)
"…by which she bound *herself*…" (NKJ, L,
M, RV)
"…by which she obligated *herself*…" (NIV)
"…*she made a vow*…*her vow* shall
stand…" (LV, RV)
(Numbers 30:4) (twice in this scripture)

"…wherewith she hath bound *her soul*…"
(KJ)
"…by which she bound *herself*…" (NKJ, L,
RV)
"…by which she obligated *herself*…" (NIV)
"…*her* promise…" (LV)
"…*her* vows and pledges…" (M)

(Numbers 30:5)

"…wherewith she bound *her soul*…" (KJ)
"…by which she bound *herself*…" (NKJ, L, M, RV)
"…by which she obligates *herself*…" (NIV)
"…still committed to *her* vows…" (M)
"… *if she* takes a vow…" (LV)
(Numbers 30:6)

"…wherewith she bound *her soul*…" (KJ)
"…by which she bound *herself*…" (NKJ, L)
"…by which she obligated *herself*…" (NIV)
"…*her* vows and pledges…shall remain…" (M)
"…*her* vows and pledges shall stand…" (LV, RV)
(Numbers 30:7)

"…wherewith she bound *her soul*…" (KJ)
"…by which she bound *herself*…" (NKJ, L)
"…by which she obligates *herself*…" (NIV)
"…which obligates her…" (M)
"…*her* vow of foolish pledge…" (LV)
"…her vow which was on *her*…" (RV)
(Numbers 30:8)

"…or bound *her soul*…" (KJ)
"…or bound *herself*…" (NKJ, L, RV)
"…or obligates *herself*…" (NIV)

"…pledges *herself*…" (M)
"…*she* makes the vow…" (LV)
"…by which she bound *herself*…" (RV)
(Numbers 30:10)

"…wherewith she bound *her soul*…" (KJ)
"…by which she bound *herself*…" (NKJ)
"…bound *herself* with an oath…" (L)
"…by which she obligated *herself*…" (NIV)
"…*her*…pledge of self denial shall
remain…" (M)
"…(*her*) vow stands…" (LV)
"..all *her* vows shall stand…" (RV)
(Numbers 30:11)

"…the bond of her *soul*…" (KJ)
"…the agreement binding *her*…" (NKKJ)
"…by which she bound *herself*…" (L)
"…*her* vow…" (M, LV, RV)
(Numbers 30:12)

"…every binding oath to afflict the *soul*…"
(KJ, NKJ, L)
"…any vow *she* makes…" (NIV)
"…any vow *she* made…" (M)
"…*her* vow…" (LV)
"…any binding vow or oath to afflict
*herself*…" (RV
(Numbers 30:13)

"…one *soul* of five hundred…" (KJ)
"…*one* of every five hundred…" (NKJ, RV)
"…one *person* of every five hundred…" (L)
"…*one* out of every five hundred…" (NIV, LV)
"…one of every five hundred of the *people*…" (M)
(Numbers 31:28)

"…and keep *thy soul* diligently…" (KJ, L, RV)
"…and diligently keep *yourself*…" (NKJ)
"…and watch *yourselves* closely…" (NIV)
"…be on *your* guard…" (M)
"…(*you*) watch out. Be very careful…(LV)
(Deuteronomy 4:9)
"…in your heart and in your *soul*…" (KJ, NKJ, L, M, RV)
"…in your hearts and *minds*…" (NIV)
"…in *mind*…" (LV)
(Deuteronomy 11:18)

"…whatsoever thy *soul* lusteth after…" (KJ)
"…whatever your *heart* desires…" (NKJ)
"…whatever your *soul* may desire…" (L)
"…as much…as *you* want…" (NIV, M)
"…as much..as *you* wish…" (LV)
"…as much as *you* desire…" (RV)
(Deuteronomy 12:15)

"…because thy *soul* longeth…" (KJ)
"…because *you* long to…" (NKJ)
"…because your *soul* longs…" (L)
"…*you* crave…and say *I* would like some…" (NIV)
(Deuteronomy 12:20)

"…whatsoever thy *soul* lusteth after…" (KJ)
"…as your *heart* desires…" (NKJ)
"…whatever your *soul* may desire…" (L)
"…as much as *you* want…" (NIV)
"…you say, *"I* want"…" (M)
"…as you say, *"I* will eat…" (RV)
(Deuteronomy 12:20)

"…whatsoever thy *soul* lusteth after…" (KJ)
"…as much as your *heart* desires…" (NKJ)
"…whatever your *soul* may desire…" (L)
"…as much of them as *you* want…" (NIV)
"…as much as *you* wish…" (M)
"…as much as *you* desire…" (RV)
(Deuteronomy 12:21)

"…which friend who is *thine own soul*…" (KJ, L)
"…friend who is as *your own soul*…" (NKJ, M, RV)
"…your *closest friend*…" (NIV, LV)
(Deuteronomy 13:6)

"…whatsoever thy *soul* lusteth after…" (KJ)
"…whatever your *heart* desires…" (NKJ)
"…whatever *you* desire…" (L, RV)
"…whatever *you* like…" (NIV)
"…whatever your *heart* may desire…" (M)
(Deuteronomy 14:26)

"…whatsoever thy *soul* desireth…" (KJ)
"…whatever your *heart* desires…" (NKJ)
"…whatever *you* may desire…" (L)
"…anything *you* wish…" (NIV)]
"…whatever *your heart* may desire…" (M)
(Deuteronomy 14:26)

"…and *His soul* was grieved…" (KJ, M)
"…and *His soul* could no longer endure…"
(NKJ)
"…the *soul of Israel* was grieved…" (L)
"…and *He* could bear Israel's misery no
longer…" (NIV)
"…and *He* was grieved…" (LV)
"…and *He* became indignant…" (RV
(Judges 10:16)

"…*his soul* was vexed…" (KJ, NKJ, L, RV)
"…*he* was tired to death…" (NIV)
"…his soul was wearied…" (M)
"…he couldn't stand it…" (LV)
(Judges 16:16)

"…as *thy soul* liveth…" (KJ)
"…as *your soul* lives…" (NKJ, L)
"…as surely as *you* live…" (NIV)
"…as you live…" (M, RV)
(1 Samuel 1:26)

"…as *thy soul* liveth…" (KJ)
"…as *your soul* lives…" (NKJ, L, RV)
"…as surely as *you* live…" (NIV)
"…as you live…" (M)
 (1 Samuel 17:55)

 "…the *soul* of Jonothan…" (KJ, NKJ, L, M, RV)
"…*one in spirit* with Jonothan…" (NIV)
"…a bond of love between *them*…" (M)
(1 Samuel 18:1)

"…the *soul* of David…" (KJ, NKJ, L, M, RV)
"…loved *him* as *himself*…" (NIV)
"…a bond of love between *them*…" (M)
(1 Samuel 18:1)

"…as his *own soul*…" (KJ, NKJ, L, RV)
"…loved *him as himself*…" (NIV, M)
(1 Samuel 18:1)

"…loved him as *his own soul*…" (KJ, NKJ, L, RV)

"…loved him as *himself*…" (NIV)
"…because *he* loved *him*…" (M)
"…a bond of love between *them*…" (LV)
(1 Samuel 18:3)


"…as *thy soul* lives…" (KJ)
"…as *your soul* lives…" (NKJ)
"…as *the Lord* lives…" (L, M, RV)
"…and as *you* live…" (NIV, M, RV)
"…*I* swear…" (LV)
(1 Samuel 20:3)


"…whosoever *thy soul* desireth…" (KJ)
"…whatever *you yourself* desire…" (NKJ)
"…whatever *you* desire…" (L)
"…whatever *you* want me to do…" (NIV)
"…what do *you* want…" (M)
"…what can I do (for *you*)…" (LV)
"…whatever *you* say, I will do…" (RV)
(1 Samuel 20:4)
"…he loved him as he loved *his own
soul*…" (KJ, NKJ, L, RV)
"…he loved him as he loved *himself*…"
(NIV)
"…because of his love for *him*…" (M)
"…as much as he loved *himself*…" (LV)
(1 Samuel 20:17)


"…come…according to all the *desire of Thy
soul*…" (KJ, NKJ, L)

"…come…according to all *your heart's
desire*…" (RV)
"…come…whenever it pleases *You*…"
(NIV)
"…if *you* care to come…" (M)
"…(*you*) come on down…" (LV)
(1 Samuel 23:20)


"…yet thou huntest *my soul* to take it…"
(KJ)
"…yet you hunt *my life* to take it…" (NKJ,
RV)
"…yet you hunt *me* to take my life…" (L)
"…you are hunting me down to take *my
life*…" (NIV)
"…you intend to take *my life*…" (M)
"…you have been hunting for *my life*…"
(LV)
(1 Samuel 24:11)


"…as the Lord liveth and as *thy soul*
liveth…" (KJ)
"…as the Lord lives and as *your soul*
lives…" (NKJ, L, RV)
"…as the Lord lives and as *you* live…"
(NIV, M)
"…by the life of God and my *your own life*,
too…" (LV))
(1 Samuel 25:26)

"…and to seek *thy soul*…" (KJ)
"…and seek *your life*…" (NKJ, L, M, RV)
"…to take *your life*…" (NIV)
"…who seek your life…" (LV)
(1 Samuel 25:29)


"…the *souls* of thine enemies…" (KJ)
"…the *lives* of your enemies…" (NKJ, L,
 NIV, M, LV, RV)
(1 Samuel 25:29)



"…for *my soul* was precious…" (KJ)
"…for *my life* was precious…" (NKJ, L.
RV)
"…you considered *my life* precious…"
(NIV)
"…you held *my life* precious…" (M)
"…you saved *my life*…" (LV)
(1 Samuel 26:21)

"…the *soul of all the people* was grieved…"
(KJ, NKJ, L)
"…*each one* was bitter in spirit…" (NIV)
"…all the people were bitter in *soul*…" (RV)
"…*the people* were in an ugly mood…" (M)
"…in their bitter grief…*the men*…" (LV)
1 Samuel 30:6)

"…who has redeemed *my soul* out of all adversity…" (KJ)

"…who has redeemed *my life* from all adversity…" (NKJ)

"…who has saved *my life* out of every adversary…" (L)

"…who has delivered *me* out of all trouble…" (NIV)

(2 Samuel 4:9)


"…that are hated of David's *soul*…" (KJ, NKJ, L, RV)

"…whom the *soul* of David hates…" (M)

"…who are David's *enemies*…" (NIV)

"…how *I* hate them…" (LV)

(2 Samuel 5:8)


"…as *thy soul* liveth…" (KJ)

"…as *you* live…" (NKJ, L, NIV, RV)

"…by the life of *your soul*…" (M)

"…*I swear*…" (LV)

(2 Samuel 11:11)


"…the *soul of King David* longed to…" (KJ)

"…and *King David* longed…" (NKJ, L)

"…and *the spirit of the king* longed…" (NIV, RV)

"…and *King David's heart* longed…" (M)

"…*King David*…longed, day after day…"

(LV)
(2 Samuel 13:39)

"…as *thy soul* liveth…" (KJ)
"…as *you* live…" (NKJ)
"…as *your soul* lives…" (L)
"…as surely as *you* live…" (NIV, RV)
"…as sure as *your life*…" (M)
(2 Samuel 14:19)

"…that hath redeemed *my soul*…" (KJ)
"…that has redeemed *my life* from every distress…" (NKJ)
"…Who has saved *my soul* out of all distress…" (L)
"…Who has delivered *me* out of every trouble…"(NIV)
"…Who has redeemed *me*…" (M)
"…Who has rescued *me* from every danger…"(LV)
(1 Kings 1:29)

"…according to all *thy soul* desireth…" (KJ, L)
"…all *your heart* desires…" (NKJ)
"…all that *your heart* desires…" (NIV)
"…all that your soul desires…" (RV)
"…all that you desire…" (M)
"…and give you absolute power…" (LV)
(1 Kings 11:37)

"…let this *child's soul* come into him again…" (KJ, NKJ, L, RV)
"…let this *boy's life* return to him…" (NIV)
"…let now the life of this child return to him…" (M)
"…let this child's spirit return to him…" (LV)
(1 Kings 17:21)

"…and the *soul* of the child came into him again…" (KJ, RV)
"…and the *soul* of the child came back to him…" (NKJ)
"…and the *soul* of the boy returned to him…" (L)
"…and the boy's *life* returned to him…" (NIV)
"…and the *life* of the child returned to him…" (M)
"…and he became *alive* again…" (LV)
(1 Kings 17:22)

"…and as *thy soul* liveth…" (KJ)
"…as *your soul* lives…" (NKJ L)
"…and as *you* live…" (NIV, M)
"…*I swear* to you…" (LV)
"…as *the Lord* lives…" (RV)
"…*I swear* to God…" (LV)
"…as *you yourself* live…" (RV)

(2 Kings 2:2, 4, 6; 4:30)

"…*her soul* is vexed within her…" (KJ)
"…*her soul* is in deep distress…" (NKJ)
"…*her soul* is in bitter anguish…" (L)
"…*she* is in bitter distress…" (NIV, RV)
"…*she* is in deep anxiety…" (M)
"…something is deeply troubling *her*…" (LV)
(2 Kings 4:27)

"…*my soul* refuses to touch…" (KJ, NKJ)
"…*my soul* is weary of its troubles…" (L)
"…*I* refuse to touch it…" (NIV)
"…that are loathsome to *me*…" (M, RV)
"…*I* gag at the thought of eating it…" (LV)
(Job 6:7)

"…*my soul* chooseth strangling and death
rather than my life…"
(KJ)
"…*my* soul chooses strangling and death
rather than my body…"   (NKJ)
"…*my life* out of destruction, and my bones
out of death…" (L)
"…*I* prefer strangling and death…" (NIV)
"…*I* would prefer strangling and prefer
death…" (M)
"…*I* would rather die of strangulation…"
(LV)
(Job 7:15)

"…I would not know *my soul*…" (KJ, L)
"…I would not know *myself*…" (NKJ)
"…I have no concern for *myself*…" (NIV)
"…I do not value *my life*…" (M)
"…I despise what *I* am…"(LV)
"…I loathe *my life*…" (RV)
(Job 9:21)


"…*my soul* is weary of my life…" (KJ, L)
"…*my soul* is saddened with life…" M
"…*my soul* loathes my life…" (NKJ)
"…*I* loath my very life…" (NIV)
"…*I* am weary of living…" (LV)
"…*I* loathe my life…" (RV)
(Job 10:1)


"…in whose hand is the *soul* of every living
thing…" (KJ)
"…in whose hand is the *life* of every living
thing…" (NKJ)
"…are the *souls* of every living thing…" (L)
"…in His hand is the *life* of every
creature…" (NIV)
"…in His hand is the life of every living
thing…" (RV)
"…under His control is the *life of* all that
lives…" (M)
"…the *soul* of every living thing is in the
hand of God…" (LV)

(Job 12:10)

"…and his *soul* within him shall mourn…"
(KJ, L)
"…and his *soul* will mourn over it…" (NKJ)
"…*he*… mourns only for himself…"
(NIVV)
"…and his *soul* bemoans himself…" (M)
"…for *him* there is only sorrow and pain…"
(LV)
"…*he* mourns only for himself…
(Job 14:22)

"…if *your soul* were in *my soul's* stead…"
(KJ, NKJ)
"…I wish *you* were in *my* place…" (L)
"…if *you* were in *my* place…" (NIV, M,
RV)
"…if *you* were I and *I* were you…" (LV)
(Job 16:4)

"…how long will you vex *my soul*…" (KJ,
M)
"…how long will you torment *my soul*…"
(NKJ)
"…how long will you grieve *my soul*…" (L)
"…how long will you torment *me*…" (NIV,
RV)
"…how long are you going to trouble me…"
(LV)

(Job 19:2)


"…what *his soul* desireth…" (KJ)
"…whatever *his soul* desires…" (NKJ)
"…what *his soul* desires…" (L)
"…what *he* desires…" (RV)
"…whatever *he* pleases…" (NIV)
"…what *he* wants to do…" (M)
"…whatever *he* wants to do…" (LV)
(Job 23:13)


"…when God taketh away *his soul*…" (KJ)
"…if God takes away *his life*…" (NKJ)
"…when God takes away *his life*…" (L, NIV)
"…when God cuts him off and takes away his *soul*…" (M)
"…when God cuts him off and takes away his *life*…" (LV, RV)
(Job 27:8)


"…they pursue *my soul*…" (KJ)
"…they pursue *my honor*…" (NKJ)
"…they have pursued *my paths*…" (L)
"…*my dignity* is driven away…" (NIV)
"…*my welfare* vanishes…" (M)
"…*my prosperity* has vanished…" (LV)
"…*my honor* is pursued…" (RV)
(Job 30:15)

"…*my soul* is poured out…" (KJ, NKJ, RV)
"…*my soul* is weary…" (L)
"…*my life* ebbs away…" (NIV)
"…my soul sinks within me…" (M)
"…my heart is broken…" (LV)
(Job 30:16)

"…by wishing a curse to *his soul*…" (KJ)
"…by asking a curse on *his soul*…" (NKJ)
"…nor has *my soul* wished for any of these things…" (L)
"…*I* have not allowed my mouth to sin by invoking a curse against *his life*…"
(NIV, RV)
'…I did neither commit the sin of cursing *my enemy*…" (M)
"…I have never cursed *anyone*…" (LV)
(Job 31:30)

"…many there be who say of *my soul*…"
(KJ,L)
"…Many are they who say of *me*…" (NKJ)
"…Many are saying of *me*…" (NIV, RV)
"…Many say to *me*…" (M)
"…so many say that God will never help *me*…" (LV)
(Psalms 3:2)

"…return Oh Lord, deliver *my soul*…" (KJ.L)

"…return Oh Lord, deliver *me*…" (NKJ)
"…turn Oh Lord, and deliver *me*…" (NIV)
"…turn Oh Lord and save *my life*…" (RV
"…come Oh Lord, and make *me* well…"
(M, LV)
(Psalms 6:4)

"…lest he tear *my soul* like a lion…"(KJ, M)
"…lest they tear *me* like a lion…" (NKJ)
"…lest *my soul* be torn like a lion…" (L)
"…or they will tear *me* like a lion…" (NIV)
"…don't let them pounce upon *me* like a
lion would…" (LV)
"…lest like a lion they rend me…" (RV)
(Psalms 7:2)

"…let the enemy persecute *my soul*…" (KJ)
"…let the enemy pursue *me* and overtake
*me*…" (NKJ, L, NIV)
"…let my enemies destroy *me*…" (LV)
(Psalms 7:5)

"…how say ye to *my soul*…" (KJ, NKJ)
"…how say you to *me*…" (L)
"…how can you say to *me*…" (NIV, RV)
"…how can you see *my soul*…" (M)
"…how dare you tell *me*…" (LV)
(Psalms 11:1)

"…how long shall I take counsel in *my*

*soul*…" (KJ, NKJ)
"…how long shall I keep sorrow in *my soul*…" (L)
"…how long must I wrestle with *my thoughts*…" (NIV)
"…how long shall I keep planning in *my soul*…" (M)
"…how long shall I keep hiding daily anguish in *my heart*…" (LV)
"…how long must I bear pain in my soul…" (RV)
(Psalms 13:2)


"…Oh *my soul*, though hast said unto the Lord…" (KJ, NKJ)
"…*I* have said unto the Lord…" (L)
"…*I* said to the Lord…" (NIV, RV)
"…*I* said to Jehovah…" (M)
"…*I* said to Him…" (LV)
(Psalms 16:2)


"…for thou wilt not leave *my soul* in hell…"(KJ)
"…for you will not leave *my soul* to shoel…"(NKJ)
"…for thou hast not left *my soul* in shoel…" (L)
"…because you will not abandon *me* to the grave…"(NIV)
"…for though dost not give *me* up to

shoel…" (RV)
(Psalms 16:10)

"…deliver *my soul* from the wicked…" (KJ,
L, M)
"…deliver *my life* from the wicked…"
(NKJ, RV)
"…rescue *me* from the wicked…" (NIV)
"…save *me* from these men of the world…"
(LV)
(Psalms 17:13)

"…deliver *my soul* from the sword…" (KJ,
L, M, RV)
"…deliver *me* from the sword…" (NKJ)"…deliver *my life*
from the sword…" (NIV)
"…rescue *me* from death…" (LV)
(Psalms 22:20)

"…none can keep alive *his own soul*…"
(KJ)
"…even he who cannot keep *himself*
alive…" (NKJ)
"…my soul is alive to Him…" (L)
"…those who cannot keep *themselves*
alive…" (NIV)
"…he who cannot keep *himself* alive…"
(RV)
"…unable to keep *his soul* alive…" (M)
(Psalms 22:29)

"…*his soul* shall dwell at ease…" (KJ)
"…*his soul* shall dwell in prosperity…" (M)
"…*he himself* shall dwell in prosperity…"
(NKJ, RV)
"…*his soul* shall abide with grace…" (L)
"…*he* will spend his days in prosperity…"
(NIV)
"…*he* shall live within God's circle of
blessings…" (LV)
(Psalms 25:13)

"…keep *my soul*…" (KJ, NKJ, L, M)
"…guard *my life*…" (NIV, RV)
"…save *me*…" (LV)
(Psalms 25:20)

"…gather not *my soul* with sinners…." (KJ,
M)
"…do not gather *my soul* with sinners…"
(NKJ)
"…destroy *me* not with sinners…" (L)
"…do not take away *my soul* with
sinners…" (NIV)
"…don't treat *me* as a common sinner…"
(LV)
"…sweep *me* not away with sinners…"
(RV)
(Psalms 26:9)

"...Thou hast brought up *my soul* from the grave..." (KJ)

"...You brought *my soul* up from the grave..." (NKJ

"...Thou has brought up *my soul* from Shoel.." (L, M, RV)

"...You brought *me* up from the grave..." (NIV)

"...You brought me back from the brink of the grave..." (LV)

(Psalms 30:3)

"...to deliver *their soul* from death..." (KJ, NKJ, L, RV)

"...to save *their souls* from death..." (M)

"...to keep *them* alive in famine..." (NIV)

"...He will keep *them* from death..." (LV)

(Psalms 33:19)

"...*our soul* waiteth for the Lord..." (KJ)'

"...*our soul* waits for the Lord..." (NKJ, L, M, RV)

"...*we* wait in hope for the Lord..." (NIV)

"...*we* can depend on the Lord..." (LV)

(Psalms 33:20)

"...the Lord redeemeth *the soul* of his servant..." (KJ)

"...the Lord redeems *the soul* of his servants..." (NKJ, L, M)

"...the Lord redeems *his servants*..." (NIV)

"...he will redeem *them*..." (LV)
"...the Lord redeems *the life* of his servants..." (RV)
(Psalms 34:22)

"...say unto *my soul*..." (KJ, NKJ, L, NIV, RV)
"...let *me* hear you say..." (LV)
(Psalms 35:3)

"...that seek after *my soul*..." (KJ, L, M)
"...who seek after *my life*..." (NKJ, RV)
"...who plot *my ruin*..." (NIV)
"...who are trying to kill *me*..." (LV)
(Psalms 35:4)

"...they have digged for *my soul*..." (KJ, M)
"...they have dug...for *my life*..." (NKJ)
"...they have dug pits for *me*..." (L)
"...dug a pit for *me*..." (NIV)
"...they laid a trap for *me*..." (LV)
"...they hid their net for *me*..." (RV)
(Psalms 35:7)

"...to the spoiling of *my soul*..." (KJ)
"...to the sorrow of *my soul*..." (NKJ)
"...they destroyed *my reputation*..." (L)
"...and leave *my soul* forlorn..." (NIV, RV)
"...bereavement has come to *my soul*..." (M)

"…*I* am sinking down to death…" (LV)
(Psalms 35:12)

"…I humbled *my soul*…" (KJ, L, M)
"…I humbled *myself*..." (NKJ)
"…and humbled *myself*…" (NIV)
"…*I* prayed for them with utmost
earnestness" (LV)
"…I afflicted *myself*…" (RV)
(Psalms 35:13)

"…rescue *my soul*…" (KJ, L)
"…rescue *me*…" (NKJ)
"…rescue *my life*…" (NIV)
(Psalms 35:17)

"…that seek after *my soul* to destroy it…"
(KJ, L, M)
"…who seek to destroy *my life*…" (NKJ)
"…who seek to take *my life*…" (NIV)
"…all those who seek to destroy *me*…"
(LV)
"…who seek to snatch away *my life*…"
(RV)
(Psalms 40:14)

"…heal *my soul*…" (KJ, L, NKJ, M)
"…heal *me*…" (NIV, LV, RV)
(Ps 41:4)

"…for *our soul* is bowed down to the dust…" (KJ, NKJ, M, RV)
"…for *our soul* is humbled down to the dust…" (L)
"…*We* are brought down to the dust…" (NIV)
"…*we* lie face downward…" (LV)
(Psalms 44:25)


"…for the redemption of their *souls* is precious…" (KJ, L, NKJ)
"…the ransom for a *life* is costly…" (NIV)
"…for such redemption of their *life*…" (M)
"…a *soul* is far too precious to be ransomed…" (LV)
"…for the ransom of his *life*…" (RV)
(Psalms 49:8)


"…but God will redeem *my soul*…" (KJ, L, NKJ, M, LV)
"…but God will ransom *my soul*…" (RV)
"…but God will redeem *my life*…" (NIV)
(Psalms 49:15)


"…while he lived, he blessed *his soul*…" (KJ, M)
"…while he lives, he blesses *himself*…" (NKJ)
"…while he lived, *he* lived comfortably…" (L)

"…while he lived, he counted *himself* blessed…"(NIV)

"…man calls *himself* happy all through his life…"(LV)

"…while he lives, he calls *himself* happy…" (RV

(Psalms 49:18)


"…and oppressors seek after *my soul*…" (KJ)

"…and oppressors have sought after *my life*…"(NKJ)

"…strangers are attacking *me*…" (NIV)

"…and violent men seek *my life*…" (M)

"…violent men have risen against *me*…" (LV)

"…insolent men have risen against *me*…" (RV)

(Psalms 54:3)

"…the Lord is with them that uphold *my soul*…" (KJ)

"…the Lord is with those who uphold *my life*…"(NKJ)

"…the Lord sustains *my soul*…" (L)

"…the Lord is the one who sustains *me*…" (NIV, M)

"…God is *my* helper…" (LV)

"…God is the upholder of *my life*…" (RV)

(Psalms 54:4)

"…He hath delivered *my soul* in peace…" (KJ)

"…He hath redeemed *my soul*…" (NKJ)

"…He ransoms *me* unharmed…" (NIV)

"…He will rescue *my soul*…" (M)

"…He will rescue *me*…" (LV)

"…He will deliver *my soul*…" (RV)

(Psalms 55:18)

"…when they wait for *my soul*…" (KJ)

"…they lie in wait for *my life*…" (NKJ)

"…they wish for *my death*…"(L)

"…eager to take *my life*…" (NIV)

"…they have waited for *my soul*…" (M)

"…waiting to kill *me*…" (LV)

"…they watch *my* steps…" (RV)

(Psalms 56:6)

"…for thou hast delivered *my so*ul…" (KJ, L, NKJ, M, RV)

"…for you have delivered *me*…" (NIV)

"…you have saved me from death…" (LV)

(Psalms 56:13)

"…*my soul* is among lions…" (KJ, NKJ, M)

"…*I* am among lions…" (NIV)

"…*I* am surrounded by fierce lions…" (LV)

"…*I* lie in the midst of lions…" (RV)

(Psalms 57:4)

"…they have digged a pit for *me*…" (KJ)
"…they have dug a pit before *me*…" (NKJ)
"…they dug a pit in *my* path…" (NIV)
"…they have digged a pit for *my soul*…"
(L)
"…they have prepared a net for my steps…"
(M, RV)
"…(they) have set a trap for me…" (LV)
 (Psalms 57:6)

"…for they lie in wait for my *soul*…" (KJ)
"…for they lie in wait for my *life*…" (NKJ,
M, RV)
"…lo, they lie in wait for my *soul*…" (L)
"…they lie in wait for *me*…" (NIV)
"…they lurk in ambush for my life…" (LV)
(Psalms 59:3)

 "…they seek *my soul*…" (KJ, L)
"…they seek *my life*…" (NKJ, NIV)
"…those who seek to ruin *my soul*…" (M)
"…those plotting to destroy *me*…" (LV)
"…those who seek to destroy *my life*…"
(RV)
(Psalms 63:9)

"…who hold *our soul* in life…" (KJ, L)
"…who keeps *our soul* among the living…"
(NKJ)
"…He has preserved *our lives*…" (NIV)

"…who seek our soul in *life*…" (M)
"…who holds *our lives* in His hand…" (LV)
"…who has kept us among *the living*…"
(RV)
(Psalms 66:9)


"…I will declare what He has done for *my soul*…" (KJ, L, NKJ, M)
"…let me tell you what He had done for *me*…" (NIV
"…I will tell you what he did for *me*…"
(LV, RV)
(Psalms 66:16)


"…for the waters are come into *my soul*…"
(KJ)
"…where the floods overflow *me*…" (L)
"…for the waters have come up to *my* neck…" (NKJ, NIV, RV)
"…for the waters come up to *my* lips…"
(M)
"…the waters rise around *me*…" (LV)
(Psalms 69:1)


"…draw near unto *my soul* and redeem *it*…" (KJ, L, NKJ)
"…draw near to *me*, redeem *me*…" (RV)
"…come near and rescue *me*, redeem *me*…"
(NIV)
"…come near to me…" (M)

"…come Lord and rescue me…" (LV)
(Psalms 69:18)

"…that seek after *my soul*…" (KJ, L, M)
"…that seek *my life*…" (NKJ)
"…those who seek *my life*…" (NIV, RV)
"…(those) who are after *my life*…" (LV)
(Psalms 70:2)

"…they that lie in wait for *my soul*…" (KJ, L)
"…those who lie in wait for *my life*…" (NKJ)
"…those who wait to kill *me*…" (NIV)
(Psalms 71:10)

"…that are adversaries to *my soul*…" (KJ)
"…those who are adversaries of *my life*…" (NKJ)
"…who envy *my soul*…" (L)
"…those who want to harm *me*…" (NIV)
"…those who watch *my life*…" (M)
"…those who watch for *my life*…" (RV)
"…my enemies are whispering (about *me*)…" (LV)
(Psalms 71:13)

"…my *soul* which thou hast redeemed…"
    (KJ, L, NKJ, M, RV)
"…*I,* whom you have redeemed…" (NIV)

"…for redeeming *me*…" (LV)
(Psalms 71:23)

"…He shall redeem *their souls*…" (KJ, L, M, LV)
"…He will redeem *their life*…" (NKJ)
"…He will rescue *them*…" (NIV)
"…He redeems *their life*…" (RV)
'…He shall redeem *their soul*…" (M)
"…He will save *them*…" (LV)
(Psalms 72:14)

"…*the soul* of thy turtle dove…" (KJ, RV)
"…the *life* of your turtle dove…" (NKJ, M)
"…*the soul* that confesses to thee.." (L)
"…*the life* of your dove…" (NIV)
'…save *me,* protect your turtle dove…"
(LV)
(Psalms 74:19)

"…He spared not *their souls* from death…"
(KJ, L)
"…He did not spare *their souls* from death…" (NKJ, M)
"…He did not spare *them* from death…"
(NIV)
"…He did not spare the *Egyptians* lives…"
(LV)
(Psalms 78:50)

"...preserve *my soul*..." (KJ, L)
"...preserve *my life*..." (NKJ, RV)
"...Guard *my life*..." (NIV)
"...O, keep *my* life..." (M)
"...protect *me* from death..." (LV)
(Psalms 86:2)

"...rejoice the *soul of Thy servant*..." (KJ, L, NKJ)
"...gladden the *soul* of Thy servant..." (M, LV)
"...bring joy to *Your servant*..."
"...give *me* happiness..." (LV)
(Psalms 86:4)

"...Thou hast delivered *my soul*..." (KJ, L, NKJ, RV)
"...You have delivered *me*..." (NIV)
"...Thou didst rescued *my soul*..." (M)
"...You have rescued *me*..." (LV)
(Psalms 86:13)

"...violent men has sought after *my soul*.."
(KJ, L)
"...violent men have sought *my life*..."
(NKJ)
"...the arrogant are attacking *me*..." (NIV)
"...a gang of brutal men seek *my life*..."
(M)
"...violent, Godless men are trying to kill

*me...*" (LV)
"...a band of ruthless men seek *my life*..."
(RV)
(Psalms 86:14)

"...why castest Thou off *my soul*..." (NKJ)
"...forsake not *my soul*..." (L)
"...why...do You reject *me*..." (NIV)
"...why...dost Thou reject *my soul*..." (M)
"...why have You thrown *my life* away..."
(LV)
"...why hast Thou swept over *me*..." (RV)
(Psalms 88:14)

"...deliver *his soul*..." (KJ, L, M, RV)
"...can he deliver *his life*..." (NKJ)
"...can...he save *himself*..." (NIV)
"...can rescue *his life*..." (LV)
 (Psalms 89:48)

"...*my soul* had almost dwelt in silence..."
(KJ, NKJ,RV)
"... *my soul* would soon have dwelt in
silence..." (M)
"...*my soul* would soon have been in
trouble..." (L)
"...*I* would soon have dwelt in the silence of
death..." (NIV)
"...*I* would have died..." (LV)
(Psalms 94:17)

"…they gather themselves together against the *soul*…" (KJ)
"…they gather together against the *life* of the righteous…"(NKJ)
"…they lay snares to trap the *soul*…" (L)
"…they band together against the *righteous*…" (NIV)
"…they joined forces against the life…" (M, RV)
"…those who condemn the *innocen*t to death…" (LV)
(Psalms 94:21)

"…hungry and thirsty, *their soul* fainted in them…" (KJ, L, NKJ)
"…hungry and thirsty and *their lives* ebbed away…"(NIV)
"…hungry and thirsty, *their souls* became faint…" (M, LV, RV)
(Psalms 107:5)

"…for He satisfied *the longing soul*… and fills *the hungry soul* with goodness…"(KJ, L, NKJ)
"…for He satisfies *the thirsty*…and fills *the hungry* with good things…" (NIV)
"…for He satisfies the *thirsty soul*… and fill the hungry with good…" (M, LV)
"…for He satisfies *him* who is thirsty,

and the hungry He fill with good things…" (RV)
(Psalms 107::9)

"…*their souls* abhorred all manner of
food…" (KJ, L, NKJ)
"…*they* loathed all food…" (NIV, RV)
"…to *them*, their food became abhorrent…"
(M)
"…*their* appetites were gone…" (LV)
(Psalms 107:18)

"…their *soul* is melted because of
trouble…" (KJ, NKJ)
"…their *soul* is troubled within them…" (L)
"…*their* courage melted away…" (NIV, M)
"…the *sailors* cringe in terror…" (LV)
"…*they* went down to the depths…" (RV)
(Psalms 107:26)
"…and of them that speak evil against *my
soul*…" (KJ)
"…and to those who speak evil against *my
person*…" (NKJ)
"…and if those who speak evil against
*me*…" (L)
"…to those who speak evil of *me*…" (NIV)
(Psalms 109:20)

"…to save him from those who condemn *his
soul*…" (KJ)
"…to save him from those who condemn

208

*him…*" (NKJ)
"…to save *his soul* from judgment…" (L)
"…to save *his life* from those who condemn him…"(NIV)
(Psalms 109:31)

"…deliver *my soul*…" (KJ, L, NKJ)
"…save *me…* " (NIV)
(Psalms 116:4)

"…*my soul* cleaveth unto the dust…" (KJ, L, NKJ)
"…*I* am laid low in the dust…" (NIV)
(Psalms 119:25)

"…*my soul* is continually in my hand…" (KJ, NKJ)
"…*my soul* is continually in thy hands…" (L)
"…I constantly take *my life* in my hands…"(NIV)
(Psalms 119:109)

"…thy testimonies are wonderful, therefore doth *my soul* keep them…" (KJ, L, NKJ)
"…your statutes are wonderful, therefore *I* obey them…" (NIV
(Psalms 119:129)

"...*my soul* hath kept Thy testimonies..."
(KJ, L, NKJ, M)
"...*I* obey your statutes..." (NIV)
"...*I* have looked for your
commandments..." (LV)
"...*my soul* keeps Thy testimonies..." (RV)
(Psalms 119:167)

"...let *my soul* live...:" (KJ, L, NKJ, M)
"...let *me* live..." (NIV, LV, RV)
(Psalms 119:175)

"...deliver *my soul*, O Lord..." (KJ, L, NKJ)
"...save *me*, O Lord..." (NIV)
"...deliver *me*..." (M, LV, RV)
(Psalms 120:2)

"...*my soul* has long dwelt..."(KJ,L,NKJ)
"...too long have *I* lived..." (NIV)
"...*my soul* has lived..." (M)
"...*my* troubles pile high..." (LV)
"...too long have *I*..." (RV)
(Psalms 120:6)

"...He shall preserve *thy soul*.." (NK)
"...the Lord shall preserve *you* from all
evil..." (NKJ)
"...He will preserve *your soul*..." (L, M)
"...The Lord will keep *you* from all

harm…" (NIV)
"…and preserve *your life*…" (LV)
"…He will keep *your life*…" (RV)
(Psalms 121:7)


"…*our soul* is exceedingly filled with the
scorning…" (KJ, NKJ)
"…*our soul* has enough of the scorn…" (L)
"…*we* have endured much ridicule…"
(NIV)
"…*our souls* have had more than enough…"
(M)
"…*we* have had our fill…" (LV)
"…too long *our souls* have been…" (RV)
(Psalms 123:4)


"…the stream had gone over *our soul*…"
(KJ)
"…then the waters would have
overwhelmed *us*…" (NKJ)
"…the stream would have gone over *us*…"
(L)
"…the torrent would have swept over *us*…"
(NIV)
"…*we* would have been drowned…" (LV)
"…the flood would have swept *us* away…"
(RV)
(Psalms 124:4)


"…the proud waters had gone over *our*

*soul...*" (KJ)

"...the swollen waters would have gone over *our souls...*" (NKJ, M)

"...the great waters would have gone over *us...*" (L)

"...the raging waters would have swept *us* away..." (NIV)

"...the torrent would have gone over *us...*" (RV)

(Psalms 124:5)

"...*our soul* has escaped as a bird..." (KJ, NKJ, L, M)

"...*we* have escaped like a bird..." (NIV, RV)

"...*we* have escaped with our lives..." (LV)

(Psalms 124:7)

"...*my soul* doth wait..." (KJ)

"...*my soul* waits..." (L, RV)

"...*I* wait for the Lord..." (NKJ, NIV)

"...my soul is in expectation..." (M)

"...I wait expectantly..." (LV)

(Psalms 130:5)

"...*my soul* waits for the Lord..." (KJ, NKJ, NIV, RV)

"...*I* have waited for the Lord..." (L)

"...my soul is looking for the Lord..." (M)

"...I long for Him..." (LV)

(Psalms 130:6)

"…with strength in *my soul…*"(KJ, M)
"…and did increase the strength of *my soul……*" (NKJ, L)
"…You made *me* bold and stouthearted…" (NIV)
"…giving *me* the strength *I* need…" (LV)
"…*my* strength of *soul* you did increase…" (RV)
(Psalms 138:3)

"…and *that, my soul* knowest…" (KJ, MKJ,L)
"…and *that I* know full well…" (NIV)
"…as *my soul* is well aware…" (M)
"…how well *I* know it…" (LV)
"…Thou knowest *me* right well…" (RV)
(Psalms 139:14)

"…leave not *my soul* destitute…" (KJ,
"…do not leave *my soul* destitute…" (NKJ)
"…do not give *me* over to death…" (NIV)
"…do not pour out *my life*…" (M)
"…don't let them slay *me*…" (LV)
"…leave *me* not defenseless…" (RV)
(Psalms 141:8)

"…no man cared for *my soul*…" (KJ, L)
"…no one cares for *my soul*…" (NKJ)

"…no man cares for *my life*…" (NIV)
"…no man cares for *me*…" (RV)
"…no one seeks *my* welfare…" (M)
"…no one cares a bit what happens to
*me*…" (LV)
(Psalms 142:4)

"…Bring *my soul* out of prison…" (KJ,
NKJ,L)
"…Set *me* free from my prison…" (NIV)
"…lead out *my soul* from its prison…" (M)
"…bring *me* out of prison…" (LV, RV)
(Psalms 142:7)

"…for the enemy has persecuted *my soul*…"
(KJ,NKJ,L)
"…for the enemy has hunted after *my
soul*…" (M)
"…the enemy pursues *me*…" (NIV)
"…my enemy has pursued *me*…" (RV)
"…my enemies chased and caught *me*…"
(LV)
(Psalms 143:3)

"…bring *my soul* out of trouble…"
(KJ,NKJ,L)
"…bring *me* out of trouble…" (NIV, LV)
"…preserve *my life*…" (M, RV)
(Psalms 143:11)

"…destroy all those that afflict my *soul*…"
(KJ,NKJ)
"…destroy all the enemies of my *soul*…"
(L)
"…destroy all *my* foes…" (NIV)
"…silence *my* foes…" (M)
"…cut off all *my* enemies…" (LV)
"…destroy all *my* adversaries…" (RV)
(Psalms 143:12)

"…So shall they be life unto *thy soul*…"
(KJ, NKJ ,L)
"…they shall be life to *your soul*…" (M,
RV)
"…they will be life for *you*…" (NIV)
"…they will fill *you*…" (LV)
(Proverbs 3:22)

"…do not despise a thief if he steals to
satisfy *his soul* when *he* is hungry…"
(KJ)
"…do not despise a thief if *he* steals to
satisfy *himself* when he is hungry…"
(NKJ, RV)
"…he steals to satisfy *himself* when *he* is hungry…" (L)
"…do not despise a thief when *he* steals to satisfy *his*
hunger…"
(NIV)
"…a thief is not despised if *he* steals to
satisfy *his* vital need when *he* is

hungry…" (M)

"…excuses might even be found for a thief
if *he* steals when *he* is starving…"
(LV)
(Proverbs 6:30)

"…he that doeth it destroyeth his own
*soul*…" (KJ)
"…he that does so destroys his own *soul*…"
(NKJ)
"…he destroys his own *soul*…" (L, LV)
"…whoever does so, destroys *himself*…"
(NIV, RV)
"…he who does it is destroying *himself*…"
(M)
(Proverbs 6:32)

"…wrongeth *his own soul*…"(KJ)
"…wrongs *his own soul*…" (NKJ)
"…wrong *their own soul*…"(L)
"…harms *himself*…" (NIV)
"…does violence to *his own soul*…" (M)
"…has injured *himself*…" (LV, RV)
(Proverbs 8:36)

"…the Lord will not suffer the *soul* of the
righteous to famish…"
(KJ,L)
"… the Lord will not allow the righteous

*soul* to famish…"(NKJ)

"…the Lord does not let *the righteous* to go hungry…"(NIV, M, RV)

"…the Lord will not let the good *man* starve to death…" (LV)

(Proverbs 10:3)

"…The merciful man doeth good to *his own soul*…(KJ,NKJ)

"…a pious man does good to *his soul*…"
(L)

"…a kind man benefits *himself*…"(NIV, RV)

"…a kindly man does *himself* good…" (M)

"…*your own soul* is nourished when you are kind…" (LV)

(Proverbs 11:17)

"…the liberal *soul* shall be made fat…" (KJ,

"…the generous *soul* will be made rich…"
(NKJ)

"…the liberal *soul* shall be enriched…" (L)

"…a liberal *man* shall be enriched…" (RV)

"…a generous *man* will prosper…" (NIV)

"…the charitable *soul* will be enriched …"
(M)

"…the liberal *man* will be rich…" (LV)
 (Proverbs 11:25)

"…but the *soul* of the transgressors shall

violence… (KJ)

"…but the *soul* of the unfaithful feeds on
violence…" (NKJ)

"…but the *souls* of the wicked shall
perish…"(L)

"…but the *unfaithful* have a craving for
violence…" (NIV)

"…but the desire of the *treacherous* is for
violence…" (M, RV)

"…the *evil minded* only wants to fight…"
(LV)

(Proverbs 13:2)


"…the *soul* of the sluggard desireth but hath
 nothing; but the *soul* of the diligent
shall be made fat…" (KJ)

"…the *soul* of a lazy man desires but has
nothing; but the *soul* of the diligent
shall be made rich… "(NKJ, M)

"…a *sluggard* is always craving; but the
*soul* of the diligent shall be enriched.."
(L)

"…the *sluggard* craves and get nothing, but
the desires of the *diligent* are full
satisfied…" (NIV)

"…the *soul* of the sluggard craves and get
nothing, while the *soul* of the diligent
is richly supplied…" (RV)

'…lazy *people* want much but get little,
while the *diligent* are prospering…"

(LV)
(Proverbs 13:4)

"...the righteous eateth to the satisfying of his *soul*..."(KJ,NKJK)
'...the *righteous* eats to satisfy *his* needs..."
(M)
"...the righteous *man* eats and is satisfied..." ..."(L)
"...the righteous eat to *their* hearts content..." (NIV)
"...the good *man* eats to live..." (LV)
"...the *righteous* has enough to satisfy *his* appetite..." (RV)
(Proverbs 13:25)

"...he that refuseth instruction despiseth *his own soul*..."(KJ)
"...he who disdains instruction despises *his own soul*..." (NKJ)
"...he who refuses instruction despises *his own soul*..." (L)
"...he who ignores discipline despises *himself...*" (NIV)
"...he who ignores correction despises *himself*..." (M)
"...he who ignores instruction despises *himself*..."(RV)
"...to reject criticism is to harm *yourself*..."
(LV)

(Proverbs 15:32)

"…he that keepeth his way preserveth *his soul*…" (KJ)
"…he who keeps is way preserves *his soul*…" (NKJ)
"…he who is careful of *his soul,* safeguards his way…" (L)
"…he who guards his way guards *his life*…" (NIV)
"…he who guards his way preserves *his life*…" (RV)
"…he who guards *his life* takes heed to his way…" (M)
"…he who follows that path (*he*) is safe…" (LV)
(Proverbs 16:17)

"…that the *soul* be without knowledge, it is not good…" (KJ)
"…it is not good for a *soul* to be without knowledge…"(NKJ)
"…he who has no knowledge of his own *soul*, it is not good…(L)
"…it is not good (for *anyone*) to have zeal without knowledge…"(NIV)
"…it is not good (for *anyone)* to be ignorant…"(M)
"…it is dangerous and sinful (for *anyone*) to rush into the unknown…" (LV)

"...it is not good for a *man* to be without knowledge..." (RV)
(Proverbs 19:2)

"...an idle *soul* shall suffer hunger..." (KJ, RV)
"...an idle *person* shall suffer hunger..." (NKJ, M)
"...a proud *man* shall suffer hunger..." (L)
"...the shiftless *man* goes hungry..." (NIV)
"...a lazy *man*...goes hungry..." (LV)
(Proverbs 19:15)

"...he that keepeth the commandment keepeth *his own soul*...(KJ)
"...he that keeps the commandments keeps *his soul*..." (NKJ, M)
"...he who keeps the commandments keeps *his life*..." (RV)
"...he who keeps the law keeps *his soul*..." (L)
"...he who obeys instructions guards *his life*..." (NIV)
"...keep the commandments and keep *our life*..." (LV)
(Proverbs 19:16)

"...do not let *thy soul* spare for his crying..." (KJ)
"...do not set *your heart* on his

destruction…"(NKJ, M, RV)

"…let not *your soul* share his dishonor…"
(L)

"…do not be a willing *party* to his death…"
(NIV)

"…*you* will ruin his life…" (LV)
(Proverbs 19:18)

"…sinneth against *his own soul*…"(KJ)

"…sins against *his own life*…"(NKJ,L)

"…forfeits *his life*…" (NIV, RV)

"…endangers *his own life*…" (M)

"…is to risk *your life*…" (LV)
(Proverbs 20:2)

"…the *soul* of the wicked desireth evil…"
(KJ, NKJ, M, RV)

"…the wicked *man* craves evil…" (NIV)

"…an evil *man* loves to harm others…"
(LV)
(Proverbs 21:10)

"…keepeth *his soul* from troubles…" (KJ,
M)

"…keeps *his soul* from troubles…" (NKJ)

"…keeps *himself* from trouble…" (L, RV)

"…keeps *himself* from calamity… (NIV)

"…*you'll* stay out of trouble…" (LV)
(Proverbs 21:23)

"…and spoil the *soul* of them that spoiled them…" (KJ)

"…and plunder the *soul* of those who plunder them…" (NKJ)

"…and will plunder *those* that plunder them…" (NIV)

"…and will take the *life* of those killing them…" (M)

"…if you injure *them*, he will punish you…" (LV)

"…and despoil the *life* of those who despoil them…" (RV)

(Proverbs 22:23)


"…and get a snare to *thy soul*…" (KJ, NKJ)

"…and find a stumbling block to *your soul*…" (L)

"…and get *yourself* ensnared…" (NIV)

"…and get *yourself* in a snare…" (M)

"…and entangle *yourself* in a snare…" (RV)

"…and endanger *your soul*…" (LV)

(Proverbs 22:25)


"…and He that keepeth *thy soul*, does He not know it…" KJ,NKJ)

"…and He who keeps *your soul* knows it…" (L)

"…does not He who guards *your life* know it…" (NIV)

"…and He who watches over *your soul*…"

(M, RV)
"...God...who knows *all hearts*..." (LV)
(Proverbs 24:12)

"...for he refreshes the *soul* of his master..."
(KJ,NKJ,L, M)
"...for he refreshes the *spirit* of his
master..." (NIV, RV)
(Proverbs 25:13)

"...the full *soul* loatheth an honeycomb..."
(KJ)
"...*He* whose appetite is satisfied disdains a
honeycomb..." (M)
"...a satisfied *soul* loathes the
honeycomb..." (NKJ)
"...a *person* who is full loathes a
honeycomb; (L)
"...*he* who is full loathes honey...(NIV)
"...even honey seems tasteless to a *man*
who is full..." (LV)
"...*he* who is sated loathes honey..." (RV)
"...to the hungry *soul*, every bitter thing is
sweet..." (KJ)
"...to *him* who is hungry, every bitter thing
is sweet..." (LV, RV)
"...if *he* is hungry, *he'll* eat anything..."
(LV)
"...to a hungry *soul* every bitter thing is
sweet..."(NKJ)

"...to a hungry *person* even a bitter thing is sweet..."(L)

"...to *the hungry*, even what is bitter tastes sweet..."(NIV)

(Proverbs 27:7)


"...but the just seek *his soul*..." (KJ)

"...but the upright) seek *his well-being*..." (NKJ)

"...but the righteous) have compassion upon *them*..." (L)

"...but the upright seek his *life*..." (M)

"...a wise *man* holds his temper..." (LV)

"...but the wicked seek *his life*... " (RV)

(Proverbs 29:10)


"...hateth his own *soul*..." (KJ)

"...hates his own *life*... " (NKJ, RV)

"...hates his own *soul*..." (L)

"...is his own *enemy*..." (NIV)

"...hates *himself*..." (M)

"...must really hate *himself*..." (LV

(Proverbs 29:24)


"...and that he should make his *soul* enjoy good in his labour... (KJ, NKJ, L, M)

"...than to enjoy his food and drink..." (LV)

"...and find satisfaction in *his* work..." (NIV)

"...than to find enjoyment in *his*

toil..."(RV)
(Ecclesiastes 2:24)

"...bereaving *my soul* of good..." (KJ)
"...deprive *myself* of good..." (NKJ)
"...denying *myself* good things..." (L)
"...depriving *myself* of enjoyment..." (NIV, M)
"...depriving *myself* of pleasure..." (RV)
"...*I*...giving up so much..." (LV)
(Ecclesiastes 4:8)

"...he wanteth nothing for his *soul*..." (KJ)
"...he lacks nothing for *himself*..." (NKJ, M)
"...he lacks nothing for *his soul*..." (L)
"...he lacks nothing *his heart* desires..." (NIV)
"...they can have everything *they* want..." (LV)
"...he lacks nothing of all that *he* desires..." (RV)
(Ecclesiastes 6:2)

"...and *his soul* be not filled..." (KJ, L)
"...*his soul* is not satisfied..." (NKJ, M)
"...and *he* cannot enjoy..." (NIV)
"...but *he* does not enjoy..." (RV)
"...but (he) leaves so little..." (LV)
(Ecclesiastes 6:3)

"...*my soul* seeketh..." (KJ)
"...*my soul* still seeks..."(NKJ)
"...*my soul* sought..." (L)
"...*I* was still searching..." (NIV)
"...*my heart* sought..." (M)
"...*I* came to this result..." (LV)
"...*my mind* has sought..." (RV)
(Ecclesiastes 7:28)

"...whom *my soul* loveth..." (KJ)
"...whom *I* love..." (NKJ)
"...whom *my soul* loves..." (L, RV)
"...whom *I* love..." (NIV)
"...deep in *my soul* I love..." (M)
"...O one *I* love..." (LV)
(Solomon 1:7)

"...I sought him whom *my soul* loveth..."
(KJ)
"...I sought the one *I* love..." (NKJ)
"...I sought him who *my soul* loves..." (L)
"...I looked for the one *my heart* loves..."
(Solomon 3:1)

"...whom *my soul* loveth..."(KJ)
"...seek the one *I* love..." (NKJ, LV)
"...*my soul* loves..." (L, M, RV)
"...the one *my heart* loves..." (NIV)
(Solomon 3:2)

"…saw ye him whom *my soul* loveth?…"
(KJ)
"…have you seen the one *I* love?…" (NKJ)
"…have you seen him whom *my soul*
loves?…"(L, M)
"…have you seen the one *my heart*
loves?…(NIV)
(Solomon 3:3)

"…whom *my soul* loveth…" (KJ)
"…the one *I* love…" (NKJ, LV)
"…whom *my soul* loves…" (L, M, RV)
"…the one *my heart* loves…" (NIV)
(Solomon 3:4)

"…*my soul* failed when he spake…" (KJ,
 M, RV)
"…*my heart* leaped up when he spoke…"
(NKJ)
"…*my heart* failed when he spoke…" (L)
"…*my heart* sank at his departure…" (NIV)
"…*my heart* stopped…" (LV)
(Solomon 5:6)

"…*my soul* made me like the chariots of
Amminadib…"(KJ)
"…*my soul* had made me as the chariots of
my noble people…(NKJ)
"…*I* sat in the public chariot which was

ready…" (L)
"…*my desires* set me among the royal chariots of my people…"(NIV)
"…*my soul's* fancy seated me in a princely chariot…" (M)
"…*my fancy* set me in a chariot beside my prince…" (RV)
"…*I* was stricken with terrible homesickness…" (LV)
(Solomon 6:12)

"…woe unto *their soul*…" (KJ, NKJ, L)
"…woe to *them*…" (NIV, M, RV)
"…what a catastrophe! *They* have doomed themselves…" (LV)
(Isaiah 3:9)

"…the desire of our *soul*…" (KJ, NKJ, L, RV)
"…the desire of our *hearts*…" (NIV)
"…our *hearts* desire…" (M, LV)
(Isaiah 26:8)

"…and *his soul* is empty…" (KJ)
"…and his *soul* is still empty…"(NKJ)
"…and he is weary and famished…" (L)
"…and *his hunger* remains…" (NIV)
"…with *his hunger* unsatisfied…" (M, RV)
"…but (*a man*) is still hungry…" (LV)
"…and *his soul* has appetite…" (KJ

"…and *his soul* still craves…" (NKJ)
"…and *his thirst* not quenched…" (L, RV)
"…with *his thirst* unquenched…" (NIV)
"…*he* is faint and craving…" (M, LV))
(Isaiah 29:8)


"…to make *empty the soul of the
hungry*…" (KJ, L)
"…to *keep the hungry unsatisfied*…"
(NKJ)
"…*the hungry he leaves empty* …" (NIV)
"…*starving the soul* of the hungry…" (M)
"…an *evil man*…their *cheating of the
hungry*…" (LV)
 (Isaiah 32:6)


"…in love for *my soul* delivered it…" (KJ)
"…lovingly delivered *my soul*…" (NKJ)
"…lovingly delivered *me*…" (M, LV)
"…in your love you kept *me*…" (NIV)
"…thou has cast *my sins* behind my
back…" (RV)
(Isaiah 38:17)


"…in whom *My soul* delighteth…" (KJ)
"…in whom M*y soul* delights…" (NKJ, L,
M, RV)
"…My chosen One in whom *I* delight…"
(NIV)
"…in whom *I* delight…" (LV)

(Isaiah 42:1)

"…he cannot deliver *his soul*…" (KJ, NKJ)
"…and cannot deliver *themselves*…" (L)
"…he cannot save *himself*…" (NIV, M)
"…he cannot bring *himself* to ask…" (LV)
"…he cannot deliver *himself*…" (RV)
(Isaiah 44:20)

"…which have said to *thy soul*…" (KJ)
"…which have said to *you*…" (NKJ)
"…who have said to *your soul*…" (L)
"…who said to *you*…" (NIV, M)
"…those who tormented *you*…" (LV)
"…of *your* tormentors…" (RV)
(Isaiah 51:23)

"…make *his soul* an offering to sin…" (KJ)
"…make *His soul* an offering for sin…"
(NKJ, M, LV)
"…*His life* as an offering for sin…" (L)
"…*His life* a guilt offering…" (NIV)
"…makes *Himself* and offering for sin…"
(RV)
(Isaiah 53:10)

"…He hath poured out *His soul* unto
death…" (KJ, NKJ, M, LV )
"…He has poured out *His life* to death…"
(L, RV)

"…He poured out *His life* into death…"
(NIV)
(Isaiah 53:12)

"…we afflicted *our soul*…" (KJ)
"…we afflicted *our souls*…" (NKJ)
"…we afflicted *ourselves*…" (L, M)
"…we humbled *ourselves*…" (NIV, RV)
"…why aren't you impressed (with what
*we've* done)…" (LV)
(Isaiah 58:3)

"…a day for a man to afflict *his soul*…"
(KJ, NKJ, L)
"…a day for a man to humble *himself*…"
(NIV, RV)
"…a day for a man to bow *his head*…" (M)
"…a man to bow down *his head*…" (LV)
(Isaiah 58:5)

"…if thou draw out thy *soul* to the
hungry…"(KJ)
"…if you extend your *soul* to the hungry…"
(NKJ)
"…if you open your *hearts* to the hungry…"
(M)
"…if you give *your* bread to the hungry…"
(L)
"…pour *yourselves* out to the hungry…"
(RV)

"…and satisfy the afflicted *soul*…" (KJ, NKJ, L)

"…spend *yourselves* in behalf of the hungry…" (NIV)

"…and (*you*) satisfy the needs of the oppressed…"

"…and (if *you*) satisfy the desires of the afflicted…" (M, RV)

"…Feed the hungry. Help those in trouble…" (LV)

(Isaiah 58:10)


"…satisfy thy *soul* in drought…" (KJ)

"…satisfy your *soul* in drought…" (K, NKJ) "…satisfy your *soul* with rich food…" (L)

"…satisfy *your* need in a sun-scorched land…" (NIV)

"…satisfy your *soul* in dry places…" (M)

"…satisfy *you* with all good things…" (LV)

"…satisfy *your* desire with good things…" (RV)

(Isaiah 58:11)


"…whereas the sword reaches into the *soul*…" (KJ)

"…whereas the sword reaches into the *heart*…" (NKJ)

"…the sword reaches into the *soul*…" (L)

"…when the sword is at our *throats*…" (NIV)

"…and the sword touches the *soul*…" (M)
"…the sword is even now poised to strike
*them* dead…" (LV)
"…whereas the sword has reached *their very
life*…" (RV)
(Jeremiah 4:10)


"…because thou hast heard, O *my soul*…"
(KJ)
"…because you have heard, Oh *my soul*…"
(NKJ)
"…because *my soul* has heard…" (L)
"…for *I* have heard…" (NIV, LV)
"…for *my soul* hears…" (M)
"…for *I* hear…" (RV)
(Jeremiah 4:19)


"…*my soul* is wearied…" (KJ)
"…*my soul* is weary…" (NKJ)
"…*my soul* faints…" (L, M)
"…*my life* is given over…" (NIV)
"…*my people* are gasping…" (LV)
…" *I* am fainting…" (RV)
(Jeremiah 4:31)


"…shall not *my soul* be avenged…" (KJ,
LV)
"…shall I not avenge *myself*…" (NKJ, L,
M, RV)
"…should I not avenge *myself*…" (NIV,

RV)
"…shall I not send *my* vengence…" (LV)
(Jeremiah 5:9, 29; 9:9)

"…lest *My soul* depart from thee…" (KJ)
"…lest *My soul* depart from you…" (NKJ)
"…lest *My soul* abhor you…" (L)
"…or *I* will turn away from you…" (NIV)
"…lest *I* be alienated from you.." (M, RV)
"…I will empty the land…" (LV)
(Jeremiah 6:8)

"…the dearly beloved of *my soul…*" (JK,
NKJ, L, M, RV)
"…the one *I* love…" (NIV)
"…*my* dearest ones…" (LV)
(Jeremiah 12:7)

"…*my soul* shall weep…" (KJ, NKJ, L, M)
"…*I* will weep…" (NIV)
"…*my breaking heart* will mourn…" (LV)
"…*my eyes* will weep bitterly…" (RV
(Jeremiah 13:17)

"…hath *thou soul* loathed Zion…" (KJ, L)
"…has *your soul* loathed Zion…" (NKJ,
RV)
"…do *you* despise Zion…" (NIV)
"…does *your soul* despise Zion…" (M)
"…do *you* abhor Jerusalem…" (LV)

(Jeremiah 14:19)
"…for they have digged a pit for *my soul*…"
(KJ, L)
"…for they have dug a pit for *my life*…"
(NKJ, M, RV)
"…they have dug a pit for *me*…" (NIV)
"…they have set a trap to kill *me*…" (LV)
(Jeremiah 18:20)

"…for He hath delivered the *soul* …" (KJ)
"…for He has delivered the *life*…" (NKJ, L,
M, RV)
"…He rescues the *life*…" (NIV, LV)
(Jeremiah 20:13)

"…and *their soul* shall be as a watered
garden…" (KJ, L, M)
"…and *their life* shall be like a watered
garden…" (LV, RV)
"…*their soul* shall be like a well watered
garden…" (NKJ)
"…*they* will be like a well watered
garden…" (NIV)
(Jeremiah 31:12)

"…the *soul of the priests* with fatness…"
(KJ, L)
"…the *soul of the priests* with
abundance…" (NKJ)

"…satisfy *the priests* with abundance…"
(NIV, RV)
"…I will feast *the priests* with
abundance…" (LV)
(Jeremiah 31:14)

"…I have satiated the *weary soul*…" (KJ,
NKJ)
"…I have satisfied the *thirsty soul*…" (L)
"…I will refresh *the weary*…" (NIV)
"…I will revive *the weary* soul…"(M)
"…I have given rest to *the weary*…" (LV)
"…I will satisfy the *weary soul*…" (RV)
(Jeremiah 31:25)

"…I have replenished every *sorrowful
soul*…" (KJ, NKJ)
"…I have replenished every *hungry soul*…"
(L)
"…I will…satisfy the faint…" (NIV)
"…every *soul* I will replenish…" (M, RV)

"…I have given…joy to all *the suffering*…"
(LV)
(Jeremiah 31:25)

"…that made us this *soul*…" (KJ)
"…who made our very *souls*…" (NKJ, M,
RV)
"…who created *soul* in us…" (L)

"…who has given us *breath*…" (NIV)
"…Almighty God *his* creator…" (LV)
(Jeremiah 38:16)

"…*thy soul* shall live…" (KJ)
"…*your soul* shall live…" (NKJ)
"…*you* will spare your life…" (L)
"…*your life* will be spared…" (NIV, M, RV)
"…you and your family shall live…" (LV)
(Jeremiah 38:17)

"…and *thy soul* shall live…" (KJ, NKJ, M)
"…and *your life* shall be saved…" (L)
"…and *your life* will be spared…" (NIV, LV, RV)
(Jeremiah 38:20)

"…and *his soul* shall be satisfied…" (KJ, NKJ, L, M)
"…and *his* (Israels) appetite shall be satisfied…" (NIV)
"…and (*Israel*) to be happy once more…" (LV)
"…and *his* (Israels) desire shall be satisfied…" (RV)
(Jeremiah 50:19)

"…deliver every man *his soul*…" (KJ)
"…everyone save *his life*…" (NKJ)

"...let every man save *his life*..." (L)
"...run for *your lives*..." (NIV)
(Jeremiah 51:6)

"...deliver every man *his soul*..." (KJ)
"...let everyone deliver *himself*..." (NKJ)
"...spare every man *his life*..." (L)
"...run for *your lives*..." (NIV)
(Jeremiah 51:45)

"...they have given their pleasant things for
meat to relieve the *soul*..." (KJ)
"...they have given their valuables for food to restore *life*..."
(NKJ)
"...they have given their precious things for
food to relieve the *soul*..." (L)
"...they barter their treasures for food to
keep *themselves* alive..." (NIV)
(Lamentations 1:11)

"...the Comforter that should relieve *my
soul*..." (KJ, L)
"...the Comforter who should restore *my
life*..." (NKJ)
"...no one is near to comfort *me*..." (NIV)
(Lamentations 1:16)

"...when *their soul* was poured out..." (KJ,
L)
"...when *their life* is poured out..." (NKJ)

"...as their lives ebb away..." (NIV, M, LV)
"...and their life is poured out..." (RV)
(Lamentations 2:12)

"...removed *my soul* far off from peace..."
(KJ, NKJ, M)
"...*my soul* has gone astray from peace..."
(L)
"...*I* have been deprived of peace..." (NIV)
"...you have taken them away (from *me*)..."
(LV)
"...*my soul* is bereft of peace ..." (RV)
(Lamentations 3:17)

"...*my soul* hath them still in
remembrance..." (KJ, M)
"...*my soul* still remembers..." (NKJ)
"...remember and restore *my life*..." (L)
"...*I* will remember them..." (NIV)
"...*I* can never forget..." (LV)
"...*my soul* continually thinks of it..." (RV)
(Lamentations 3:20)

"...saith *my soul*..." (KJ)
"...says *my soul*..." (NKJ, L, M)
"...I say to *myself*..." (NIV)
"...my *soul* claims the Lord..." (LV)
"...the Lord is *my* portion..." (RV)
(Lamentations 3:24)

"…to *the soul* that seeketh Him…" (KJ)
"…to *the soul* who seeks Him…" (NKJ, L, M)
"…to *the one* who seeks Him…" (NIV)
"…to *those* who wait for Him…" (LV, RV)
(Lamentations 3:25)

"…Thou hast pleaded the causes of *my soul*…" (KJ)
"…You have pleaded the case for *my soul*…" (NKJ)
"…Thou hast pleaded *my cause*…" (L)
"…You took up *my case*…" (NIV)
"…in the pleadings of *my soul*…" (M)
"…plead *my* case…" (LV)
"…Thou hast redeemed *my life*…" (RV)
(Lamentations 3:58)

"…thou hast delivered *thou soul*…" (KJ)
"…you have delivered *your soul*…" (NKJ, L)
"…you will have saved *yourself*…" (NIV)
"…you will have saved *your soul*…" (M)
"…but *you* are blameless…" (LV)
"…but you will have saved *your life*…"          (RV)
(Ezekiel 3:19)

"…thou hast delivered *thy soul*…" (KJ)
"…you will have delivered *your soul*…" (NKJ, L)

"…you will have saved *yourself*…" (NIV)
"…you will have saved *your soul*…" (M)
"…you will have saved *your own life*…"
(LV)
"…you will have saved *your life*…" (RV)
(Ezekiel 3:21)


"…*my soul* hath not been polluted…" (KJ)
"…I have never defiled *myself*…" (NKJ, L,
NIV, M, RV)
"…*I* have never been defiled…" (LV)
(Ezekiel 4:14)


"…he shall save *his soul* alive…" (KJ)
"…he preserves *himself* alive…" (NKJ)
"…saves *his soul* alive…" (L)
"…he will save *his life*…" (NIV, M, RV)
"…he shall save *his soul*…" (LV)
(Ezekiel 18:27)


"…and *her mind* was alienated from them…" (KJ, )
 "…and alienated *herself* from them…"
(NKJ)
"…then *her soul* abhorred them…" (L)
"…*she* turned away from them in disgust…"
(NIV, RV)
"…*she* turned from them in disgust…" (M)
"…*she* hated them…" (LV)
(Ezekiel 23:17)

"…that which *your soul* pitieth…" (KJ)
"…the delight of *your soul*…" (NKJ)
"…the cleanser of *your soul*…" (L)
"…the delight of *your eyes*…" (NIV, ML,M)
"…the strength of *your nation*…" (LV)
"…the desire of *your soul*…" (RV)
(Ezekiel 24:21)

"…shall deliver *his soul*…" (KJ)
"…will save *his life*…" (NKJ)
"…he shall deliver *his life*…" (L)
"…would have saved *himself*…" (NIV)
"…would have saved *his life*…" (M, LV, RV)
(Ezekiel 33:5)

"…but thou hast delivered *thy soul*…" (KJ)
"…but you have delivered *your soul*…"
(NKJ, L)"…but you have saved *yourself*…" (NIV)
"…but you have saved *your soul*…" (M)
"…and *you* will not be responsible…" (LV)
"…but you will have saved your life…" (RV)
(Ezekiel 33:9)

"…their bread for *their soul*…" (KJ)
"…their bread shall be for *their own life*…"
(NKJ)
"…for *their own* bread…" (L)
"…this food shall be for *themselves*…"
(NIV, LV)
"…their bread will be only for *their*

*hunger*…" (M, RV)
(Hosea 9:4)


"…the waters compassed me, even to *the soul*…" (KJ)
"…the waters encompassed me, threatening *my life*…" (M)
"…the waters surrounded me, even to *my soul*…" (NKJ)
"…the waters engulfed me, even to *the soul*…" (L)
"…the deep surrounded me, the seaweed wrapped around *my head*…" (NIV)
"…the waters closed above *me*…" (LV)
"…the waters closed in over *me*…" (RV)
(Jonah 2:5)


"…when *my soul* fainted within me…" (KJ, NKJ, L, M, RV)
"…when *my life* was ebbing away…" (NIV)
"…when *I* had lost all hope…" (LV)
(Jonah 2:7)


"…*my soul* desired…" (KJ)
"…*my soul* desires…" (NKJ, RV)
"…*my soul* craves…" (L)
"…that *I* crave…" (NIV)
"…on which *my heart* is set…" (M)
"…*I* long for it…" (LV)
(Micah 7:1)

"…*his soul*…is not upright…" (KJ, NKJ, M, RV)

"…*his soul* does not delight in iniquity…" (L)

"…*his desires* are not upright…" (NIV)

"…*wicked men* fail…" (LV)

(Habakkuk 2:4)

"…and hast sinned against *thy soul*…" (KJ)

"…and sin against *your soul*…" (NKJ)

"…caused *your soul* to sin…" (L)

"…and forfeiting *your life*…" (NIV)

"…you have forfeited *your own life*…" (M, LV, RV)

(Habakkuk 2:10)

"…the shephards…*my soul* loathed them…" (KJ, NKJ)

"…*my soul* was wearied of them…" (L)

"…and *I* grew weary of them…" (NIV)

"…*my soul* was impatient with them…" (M)

"…*I* became impatient with them…" (RV)

"…*I* became impatient with these sheep…" (LV)

(Zechariah 11:8)

"…and *their soul* also abhorred me…" (KJ, NKJ)

"…and *their souls* felt loathing against

me..." (M)
"...and *they* hated me too..." (LV)
"...and *their souls* also howled against
me..." (L)
"...*the flock* detested me..." (NIV)
"...and *they* also detested me..." (RV)
(Zechariah 11:8)

Translations from New Testament follow:

NOTE: A new translation is available *for the New Testament.
The symbol (D) will stand for the Dioglott Translation.* *

"...fear not them which kill the body, but
 are not able to kill the *soul;* but rather
fear Him which is able to destroy both
body and *soul in hell...*" (KJ, NKJ, M,
RV)
"...do not be afraid of those who kill the
body but cannot kill the *soul*. Rather,
be afraid of the One who can destroy
both *soul* and body *in hell...*" (NIV)
"...do not be afraid o those who kill the
body but cannot kill the *soul*. But
above all, be afraid of the One who can
destroy both the *soul* and the body *in
hell...*" (L)
"...be not afraid of those who can kill only your bodies – but
can't touch your *souls*! Fear only God who can destroy both
*soul*

and body *in hell…*" (LV)

"…be not afraid of those who kill the body, but cannot destroy the *life*; but rather fear Him who can utterly destroy both *life* and body *in Gehenna…*) (D)
(Matthew 10:28)

"…you will find rest for *your souls* …
"(KJ,NKJ,NIV,L,M,LV,RV)
"…and *your lives* will find a resting place…" (D)
(Matthew 11:29)

"…in whom *My soul* is well pleased…"
(KJ, NKJ, RV)
"…in whom *I* delight…" (NIV)
"…in whom *My soul* delights…" (M, LV)
"…in whom *My soul* rejoices…" (L)
"…in whom *I* take delight…, (D)
(Matthew 12:18)

"…what is a man profited, if he shall gain
the whole world, and lose *his own*
*soul?…*" (KJ, NKJ)
"…what good will it be for a man if he gains
the whole world, yet forfeits *his*
*soul…*" (NIV)
"…for how would a man be benefited, if he
 should gain the whole world and lose
*his own soul…*" (L)
"…for what advantage would a man have if
he acquires the whole     world and

forfeits *his own life*…" (M, RV, D)
"…what profit is there if you gain the whole world – and lose *eternal life*…" (LV)
(Matthew 16:26; Mk 8:36)

"…what will a man give in exchange for *his soul*…" (KJ, NKJ, MIV, L)
"…what will a man offer in exchange for *his life*…" (M)
"…what can compare to the value of *eternal life*…" (LV)
"…what shall a man give in exchange for *his life*…" (RV)
"…what will a man give in ransom for *his life*…" (D)
(Matthew 16:26; Mark 8:37)

"…with all the *soul*…" (KJ, NKJ, L,
"…with all your *heart*…" (NIV, M, LV, RV)
"…with all the *understanding*…" (D)
(Mark 12:33)

"…*My soul* magnifies the Lord…" (KJ, NKJ, L, M,
"…*My soul* glorifies the Lord…" (NIV)
"…Oh how *I* praise the Lord…" (LV)
"…*My soul* extols the Lord…" (D)
(Luke 1:46)

"…and I will say to *my soul*…" (KJ, NKJ, M, RV)
"…and I shall say to *myself*…" (L, NIV, D)
"…and I will sit back and say to *myself*…" (LV,)
(Luke 12:19)

"…*Soul*, thou hast much goods…" (KJ)
"…*Soul*, you have many goods…" (NKJ)
"…*You* have many good things…" (L)
"…*You* have plenty of good things…" (NIV)
"…*Soul,* you have much wealth…, (M )
"…*Friend*, you have enough…" (LV)
"…*Soul*, you have ample goods…" (RV)
"…*Life*, thou hast an abundance…" (D)
(Luke 12:19)

"…*thy soul* shall be required of thee…" (KJ, NKJ, RV)
"…*your life* will be demanded of you…" (L, NIV, D)
"…*your soul* will be demanded of you…" (M)
"…tonight *you* will die…" (LV)
(Luke 12:20)

"…in your patience possess ye *your souls*…" (KJ, NKJ)
"…by your patience you will gain *your*

*souls...*" (L, M)
"...standing firm you will gain *life...*"
(NIV)
"...if you stand firm, you will win *your
souls...*" (LV)
"...by your endurance you will gain *your
lives...*" (RV)
"...by your patient endurance preserve *your
lives...*" (D)
(Luke 21:19)


"...now is *my soul* troubled..." (KJ, LV,
RV, D)
"...now *my soul* is troubled..." (NKJ)
"...now *my soul* is disturbed..." (L, M)
"...now *my heart* is troubled..." (NIV)
(John 12:27)


"...thou wilt not leave *my soul* in hell..."
(KJ)
"...you will not leave *my soul* in hades..."
(NKJ)
"...you will not leave *my soul* in shoel..."
(L)
"...because thou wilt not abandon *my
soul...*" (M, RV, D)
"...you will not leave *my soul* in hell..."
(LV)
"...because you will not abandom *me* to the
grave..." (NIV)

(Acts 2:27)

"...*His soul* (Christ's) was not left in
hell..." (KJ, M)
"...*His soul* (Christ's) was not left in
hades..." (NKJ, RV, D)
"...*His soul* (Christ's) was not left in the
grave..." (L)
"...*He* (Christ) was not abandoned to the
grave...(NIV)
"...*He* (Christ) would not be abandoned to
the...dead..."(M)
(Acts 2:31)

"...there were added to them about 3000
*souls*..." (KJ, NKJ, M)
"...and about 3000 *souls* were added..." (L,
RV, D)
"...3000...*baptized* were added to their
number..."(NIV)
"...*those baptized*..were about 3000 in
all..."(LV)
(Acts 2:41)

"...fear came upon *every soul*..." (KJ, NKJ,
L, RV, D)
"...*everyone* was filled with awe..." (NIV)
"...awe fell on *every soul*..." (M)
"...a deep sense of awe was on *them all*..."
(LV)

(Acts 2:43)

"…*every soul* which will not hear…" (KJ, NKJ)
"…*every person* who will not listen…" (L)
"…*anyone* who does not listen…" (NIV)
"…*every soul* that will not listen…" (M, RV)
"…*anyone* who will not listen…" (LV)
"…*every soul* which may not hear…" (D)
(Acts 3:23)

"…were of one heart and *one soul*…" (KJ, \ NKJ)
"…were of *one soul* and one mind…" (L)
"…were of *one heart* and *one mind*…" (NIV, LV)
"…were one in heart and *soul*…" (M, RV)
"…the heart and *soul* was one…" (D))
(Acts 4:32)

"…threescore and fifteen *souls*…" (KJ)
"…seventy five *people*…" (NKJ)
"…seventy five *souls*…" (L, M, RV, D)
"…whole *family*, seventy five in all…" (NIV)
"…seventy five *persons*…" (LV)
 (Acts 7:14)
"…Confirming the *souls* of the disciples…" (KJ, D)

"…strengthening the *souls* of the disciples…" (NKJ, RV)

"…strengthening the *souls* of the converts…" (L)

"…strengthening the *disciples* and encouraging them…"(NIV)

"…reassuring the *disciples,* spiritually…" (M)

"…they helped the *believers* to grow…" (LV)

(Acts 14:22)

"…subverting your *souls*…" (KJ)

"…unsettling your *souls*…" (NKJ, L)

"…unsettling your *minds*…" (RV, D)

"…troubling your *minds*…" (NIV)

"…questioned your *salvation*…" (M, LV)

(Acts 15:24)

"…two hundred threescore and sixteen *souls*…" (KJ)

"…two hundred seventy six *persons*…" (NKJ)

"…there were 276 of *us*…" (NIV, M, LV)

"…two hundred and seventy six *persons*…" (L, RV)

"…all the *souls* were two hundred and seventy six…" (D)

(Acts 27:37)

"…upon *every soul* of man…" (KJ)
"…on every *soul of man*…" (NKJ, D)
"…for *every man*…" (L)
"…for *every human*…" (NIV)
"…to *every human soul*…" (M)
"…for *Jews and Gentiles* alike…" (LV)
"…for *every human being*…" (RV)
(Romans 2:9)

"…*every soul* be subject unto higher powers…" (KJ)
"…*every soul* be subject to the governing authorities…" (NKJ)
"…*every soul* be subject to the sovereign authorities…" (L)
"…*everyone* must submit to the governing authorities…" (NIV)
"…*every person* render obedience to govern. autho…." (M)
"…*(everyone)* obey the government…" (LV)
"…*every person* be subject to the governing authority…" (RV)
"…*every person* be subject to the superior authority…" (D)
(Romans 13:1)

"…Adam was made a *living soul*…" (KJ, L)
'…the first man became a *living being*…" (NKJ)

"...Adam became a *living being*..." (NIV, M, RV, D)

"...Adam was given a *living, human body*..." (LV)

(1 Corinthians 15:45)

"...for a record upon *my soul*..." (KJ)

"...as a witness against *my soul*..." (NKJ)

"...to God concerning *myself*..." (L)

"...God as *my* witness..." (NIV)

"...as my *soul's* witness..." (M)

"...God to witness against *me*..." (LV, RV)

"...as a witness to *my soul*..." (D)

(2 Corinthians 1:23)

"...but also *our souls*..." (KJ)

"...but also *our own lives*..." (NKJ, M, LV)

"...but even *our lives*..." (L)

"...but *our lives* as well..." (NIV)

"...but also *our own selves*..." (RV, D)

(1 Thessalonians 2:8)

"...dividing asunder of *soul and spirit*..." (KJ)

"...piercing even to the division of *spirit and soul*..." (NKJ,L,RV)

"...even to dividing *soul and spirit*..." (NIV)

"...even to dividing asunder of *soul and spirit*..." (M)

"...cutting into our innermost *thoughts and*

*desires…"* (LV)
"…cutting through even to a separation of
*Life and Breath…"* (D)
(Hebrews 4:12)


"…as an anchor of *the soul…"* (KJ, NKJ,
NIV, M, LV, RV)
"…like an anchor to *us…"* (L)
"…an anchor of the *life…"* (D)
(Hebrews 6:19)


"…*My soul* shall have no pleasure in
him…" (KJ, NKJ, L, RV)
"…*I* will not be pleased with him…" (NIV)
"…*My soul* will not be pleased…" (M)
"…*God* will have no pleasure in them…"
(LV)
"…*My soul* does not delight in him…" (D)
(Hebrews 10:38)


"…believe to the saving of *the soul…"* (KJ,
NKJ)
"…faith which restores *our souls…"* (L)
"…*those* who believe and are saved…"
(NIV)
"…those who have faith to save *their
souls…"* (M)
"…faith in Him assures *our souls'*
salvation…" (LV)
"…faith to keep their souls…" (RV)

"…faith in order to a preservation of *life*…"
(D)
(Hebrews 10:39)

"…they watch for *your souls*…" (KJ)
"…they watch out for *your souls*…" (NKJ)
"…they are watchful guardians for *your souls*…" (L)
"…watch over *your souls*…" (M, LV, RV)
"…keep watch on *your behalf*…" (D)
(Hebrews 13:17)

"…which is able to save *your souls*…"(KJ, NKJ, L,M, LV,RV, D)
"…which can save *you*…" (NIV)
(James 1:21)

"…shall save *a soul* from death…" (KJ, NKJ, L, RV, D)
"…will save *him* from death…" (NIV, M)
"…will have saved a wandering *soul* from death…" (LV)
(James 5:20)

"….salvation of *your soul*…" (KJ, NKJ, L, NIV, M, LV, RV)
"…your *salvation*…" (D)
(1 Peter 1:9)

"…ye have purified *your souls*…" (KJ,

NKJ)

"...let *your souls* be sanctified..." (L)

"...you have purified *yourselves*..." (NIV)

"...with *your souls* purified..." (M)

"...*your souls* have been cleansed..." (LV)

"...having purified *your souls*..." (RV)

"...having purified *your lives*..." (D)

(1 Peter 1:22)


"...for they fight against *your very souls*..."
(LV)

"...which war against *the soul*..." (KJ, NKJ,
L, NIV, M, RV)

"...which wage war against *the life*..." (D)

(1 Peter 2:11)


"...Shepherd and Bishop of *your souls*..."
(KJ)

"...Shepherd and Overseer of *your souls*..."
(NKJ, NIV)

"...Shepherd and Guardian of *your souls*..."
(L. M, LV, RV)

"...Shepherd and Guardian of *your lives*..."
(D)

(1 Peter 2:25)

"...eight *souls* were saved by water..." (KJ)

"...eight *souls* were saved through water..."
(NKJ)

"...eight *souls* entered into it..." (L)

"...a few *people*, eight in all, were saved..."

(NIV)
"…eight *souls* were brought safely through the water…" (M)
"…eight *persons* were saved…" (LV, RV)
"…eight *persons* were carried safely…" (D)
(1 Peter 3:20)

"…the keeping of *their souls* to *him*…" (KJ)
"…commit *their souls* to Him…" (NKJ, L)
"…commit *themselves* to their faithful Creator…" (NIV)
"…entrust *their souls* to God…" (M)
"…trust *yourself* to the God who make you…" (LV)
"…entrust *your souls* to the faithful Creator…" (RV)
"…commit *your lives* in doing good to a Faithful Creator…" (D)
(1 Peter 4:19)

"…vexed in his *righteous soul*…" (KJ, D)
"…tormented his *righteous soul*…" (NKKJ)
"…his *righteous soul* was vexed…" (L)
"…was tormented in his *righteous soul*…(NIV, RV)
"…his *upright soul* was tortured…" (M)
"…*a good man*, sick of the terrible wickedness he saw…" (LV)
(2 Peter 2:8)

259

"…beguiling *unstable souls*…" (KJ, L)
"…enticing *unstable souls*…" (NKJ)
"…seduce *the unstable*…" (NIV)
"…lure *unsteady souls*…" (M)
"…luring *unstable women*…" (LV)
"…intice *unsteady souls*…" (RV)
"…alluring *unstable souls*…" (D)
(2 Peter 2:14)


"…the *souls* of them that were slain…" (KJ, L)
"…the *souls* of those who had been slain…" (NKJ, NIV, RV)
"…the *souls* of those who had been slaughtered…" (M)
"…the *souls* of those who had been martyred…" (LV)
"…the *persons* of those who had been killed…" (D)
(Revelation 6:9)


"…every *living soul* died in the sea…" (KJ, L, D)
"…very *living creature* in the sea died…" (NKJ)
"…every *living thing* in the sea died…" (NIV, RV)
"…every *living creature* that was in the sea died…" (M)
"…*everything* in all the oceans died…"

(LV)
(Revelation 16:3)

"…and *souls* of men…" (KJ, NKJ, NIV, M,
LV)
"…and hides and *slaves*…" (L)
"…human *souls*…" (RV)
"…and *lives* of men…" (D)
(Revelation 18:13)

"…the fruit that *thy soul* lusted after…" (KJ,
L)
"…the fruit that *your soul* longed for…"
(NKJ)
"…the fruit *you* longed for…" (NIV)
"…the fruit for which *your soul* longed…"
(M, RV)
"…the fancy things that *you* loved so
much…" (LV)
"…the fruit season of *thy soul's* ardent
desire…" (D)
(Revelation 18:14)

"…the *souls* of them that were beheaded…"
(NKJ, NKJ, L, NIV, LV, RV)
"…the *souls* of them that had been slain…"
(M)
"…the *persons* of those who had been
beheaded…" (D)
(Revelation 20:4)

261

Having examined all of the times that the word(s) "soul" "souls" or "soul's" appears in the Bible, I find only that it means a mortal or mortals…a living being.

I invite anyone who believes in an immortal soul that flies off to heaven when they die to find a scripture to support such a belief.

# Addendum B
# The Old Testament Jesus

The Prophesy that Jesus would be born in Bethlehem was told in the Old Testament (OT) in Micah, Chapter 5, verse 2...and shown to have come to pass in the New Tesstament (NT) in Matthew chapter 2, verse 6; Luke chapter 2, verses 4 and 11; and in John, chapter 7, verse 42.

That He would be born of a virgin, in the OT in Isaiah 7:14, and the NT in Matthew 1:23 and Luke 1:26-31

That He would be God's first born. OT Psalm 89:27 and NT Colosians 1:15 and 18, and Revelation 19:16.

That He Would be born of the house of David, in the OT, in Isaiah 9:6-7 and Jeremiah 33:15, and in the NT in John 7:42

That He would perform Miracles, in Isaiah 35:5 of the OT and Matthew 9:27-30 and John:6-7 in the NT.

That He would arrive in Jerusalem on a donkey, the OT scripture was Zecheriah 9:9 and the NT verses in Matthew

21:5, Mark 11:7-9 and Luke 19:33-38

In the OT, in Isaiah 53:3 and Paslm 69:12, we were told that He would be rejected by Israel. We know that was true because it was confirmed in Matthew 27:30.

OT Isaiah 60:3 told us that Jesus would be accepted by the Gentiles. Acts 13:47, 48 and 26:17 of the NT confirm that that is exactly what happened.

He would be condemned to death, we learned from Daniel 9:26, and we know, from Luke 23:46 and Luke 24:26 that indeed He was.

He had to die we were told in OT Isaiah 53:11,12. NT Romans 5:21 confirmed that He did.

His death would be for our sins. OT Isaiah 53:5 told us this long before NT Romans 4:25 told us after the fact.

OT Numers 9:12 prophesys that, in spike of his brutal death, He would suffer NO broken bones, and John 19:33 and 36 tell us that He did not.

Two OT verses tell us that He woulld die by crusifiction (that He'd be pierced). They are Zachariah 12:10 and Psalms 22:16. We know, from Matthew 27:35; 20:28 and John 20:27 that this was true.

Before He was born, we knew that He would be raised from

the dead after 3 days, and we know it because OT Psalm 49:15 and Jeremiah 30:9 told us so. Sure enough, NT Matthew 12:40, Mark 16:6 and Acts 2:31 and 36 tell us, after he arrived, that those facts were correct.

Psalm 68:18 tell us that Jesus would be taken up into heaven and Jesus speaks to us, through John, from Heaven in Revelation 12:5.

From Matthew 22:44, Lune 20:42,43, 1st Corinthians 15:25 and Ephesians 1:22 of the NT, we know that Jesus sits on the right hand of his Father, God and will do so till all sin is removed from the earth. But many years before He was born, we knew that He would because we are told that in Psalm 110:1-2.,

Lots would be cast for His garments, we were told in OT Scripture at Psalm 22:18, and we are told of the actual happening in NT Matthew 27:35, Luke 23:34, and John 19:24.

The place of His birth would be told by a star. OT, Numbers 24:17; NT, Matthew 2:7.

Because of Psalm 27:12, in the OT, we knew that false witnesses would rise against him, and we know from Matthew 26:60, 61 and Mark 14:56 in the NT that they did, indeed.

OT Psalm 35:19 warned that men would hate HIm without a

reason. We know, from NT John 15:24, that they did.

Most people know that Jesus taught in Parables (see NT Matthew 13:34, 35). However, not all know that we were told in the OT, years before his birth, that He would teach in that manner (See Psalm 78:2)

He will come in the clouds! OT Daniel 7:13 told us to expect that. We were told that He did in Matthew 24:30 and 26:64; Mark 13:36 and 14:62; Luke 21:27; and Revelation 1:7 and 14:14.

God would give Jesus all authority, we are told in OT Daniel 7:14. God *gave* Jesus all authority we are told in NT Matthew 28:18, John 3:35, 1st Corinthians 15:27, Philipians 2:9-11 and Revelation 11:15.

Jesus will be God's first born, OT Psalm 89:27 tells us, and Colosians 1:15,18 and Revelation 19:16 confirm the truth of that prophey.

God would make Jesus His high priest. That we knew by OT Psalm 110:4 long before Jesus was born. NT Hebrews 5:6,10 and 6:20 confirm the truth of it.

OT Isaiah 40:3 said that Jesus would be a voice crying in the desert and NT Luke 3:3 and John 1:23 tell us that He was indeed a voice crying in the desert.
He will feed His sheep like a shepard, said OT Isaiah 40:11 and NT John 10:11, Hebrews 13:20 and 1st Peter 2:25 tell us

that He was that shepard.

OT Isaiah 42:1 and 53:11 point out that Jesus *would be* God's servant, and NT Matthew 12:18 tells us that He *was*.

Jesus would heal the blind we were told in OT Isaiah 42:7, and NT Luke 4:18 tells us of one of the incidents of that.

God promised, we are told in OT Isaiah 50:7, that God would give Jesus strength for His ordeals, and we know, through NT Luke 9:51 that God *did* give him that strength.

God would highly exhault Jesus. Told in OT Isaiah    52:13 and confirmed in NT Philipians 2:9.

We knew, because of OT Isaiah 53:3, that Jesus would be despised and rejected by men. We know, because of NT Matthew 27:30,31; Luke 18:31, 33 and 23:18; and John 1:10 and 11; that he truly was despised and rejected.

In advance we knew that Jesus would bear our griefs and sorrows through OT Isaiah 53:4 and actually, we know that He did through NT Matthew 8:17 and 1st Peter 2:24.

# Addendum C
# The Athenasian Creed

"Whoever would be saved needeth before all things to hold fast to the Catholic faith. Which faith except a man keep whole and undefiled without doubt, he will perish eternally. Now the Catholic faith is this, that we worship one God in Trinity and Trinity in Unity; neither confusing the persons nor dividing the substance, for there is one person of the Father, another of the Son, and another of the Holy Ghost. But the Godhead of the Father, and of the Son and of the Holy Ghost is all one, the glory equal, the majesty co-eternal, such as the Father is, such is the Son, and such is the Holy Ghost; The Father uncreated, the Son uncreated, the Holy Ghost uncreated; the Father infinite, the Son infinite, the Holy Ghost infinite; the Father eternal, the Son eternal, the Holy Ghost eternal; yet there are not three eternals, but one eternal; as also there are not three uncreated, not three infinites, but one infinite and one uncreated. So likewise the Father is almighty, the Son almighty, the Holy Ghost almighty; and yet there are not three almighties, but one almighty. So the Father is God, the Son God, the Holy Ghost God; and yet there are not three gods but one God. So the Father is Lord, the Son Lord, the

Holy Ghost Lord; and yet there are not three Lords, but one Lord. For like as we are compelled by the Christian verity to confess each person by himself to be both God and Lord; so we are forbidden by the Catholic religion to speak of three gods or three lords. The Father is made of none, nor created, nor begotten. The Son is of the Father alone; not made, not created, but begotten. The Holy Ghost is of the Father alone; not made, nor created, nor begotten, but proceeding.

"There is, therefore, one Father, not three Fathers; one Son, not three Sons; one Holy Ghost, not three Holy Ghosts. And in this Trinity there is no one before or after, no greater or less; but all three persons are co-eternal together, and co-equal. So that in all ways, as is aforesaid, both the Trinity is to be worshipped in Unity, and the Unity in Trinity. He that therefore would be saved, let him think thus of the Trinity. Furthermore, it is necessary to eternal salvation, that he also believe faithfully the incarnation of our Lord Jesus Christ. Now the right faith is that we believe and confess that our Lord Jesus Christ, the Son of God, is both God and man. He is God, of the substance of the Father, begotten before worlds; and He is man of the substance of His mother, born in the world; perfect man, of reasoning soul and human flesh subsisting; equal to the Father as touching His Godhead; less than the Father as touching His manhood. Who, although He be God and man, yet He is not two, but is one Christ; one, however, not by conversion of His Godhead into flesh, but by taking of manhood into God; one altogether; not by confusion of the substance, but by unity of person. For as reasoning soul and flesh is one man, so God the man is one Christ, Who suffered for our salvation, descended into hell, rose again from the dead, ascended into heaven, sat down at the right hand of the Father, from whence He shall come to judge the quick and the dead. At whose coming all men will rise again with their bodies, and shall give account for their deeds. And they that have done good will go into life eternal; they that have done evil into eternal fire. This is the Catholic faith, which except a man do faithfully and steadfastly believe, he cannot be saved."

Printed in the United States
63647LVS00002B/217-264

9 781413 765502